After she finishes the makeup, she preens a bit in front of the full-length mirror attached to the door of the bathroom. She stands in front of the mirror and she turns her body to look at her profile, her breasts and belly and ass and legs in the blue-gray stockings. Now she wants a pair of heels, and she hurries to closet to find her blue-gray suede sandals. Yes, they're perfect, and after she has the straps buckled she prances back to the mirror to see the full effect again, her body now lifted four inches by the high heels, the muscles in her calves more prominent, her legs more curvaceous.

After that she dresses in lace bikini panties and a lace bra sheer enough to show her nipples. Both bra and panties are blue because Cleo likes her in blue. Valerie thinks she looks better in red or black underwear; but if Cleo wants blue, Cleo gets blue. Valerie doesn't mind it; she's thrilled she has a lover who cares about the color of her underwear.

**Also by
RACHEL PEREZ:**

*Affinities*

# ODD
# Women

**RACHEL PEREZ**

MASQUERADE BOOKS, INC.
801 SECOND AVENUE
NEW YORK, N.Y. 10017

First Masquerade Edition 1993

First printing September 1993

ISBN 1-56333-123-3

Cover Photograph © 1993 by Robert Chouraqui

Manufactured in the United States of America
Published by Masquerade Books, Inc.
801 Second Avenue
New York, N.Y. 10017

# ONE

# Valerie

Frankie is in one of her preoccupied moods. Valerie concludes that as she lies with her head in Frankie's lap as Frankie studies some papers brought home in her briefcase. It's ten o'clock in the evening, and the TV tube is now showing the evening news with the sound off. Valerie looks at the flashing pictures on the tube, and she amuses herself attempting to discover what the people are saying. Of course it makes no difference whether you have the sound on or off; whatever the people are saying is ridiculous anyway. With a sigh, Valerie slips her hand into Frankie's lap. Her fingertips tease the seam of Frankie's jeans. But nothing happens. She might as well be touching a stone statue for all the response she gets. Frankie's mind seems totally occupied with her paperwork, no evidence at all that Frankie is aware of Valerie's hand. No evidence before the bar, Valerie thinks. She

7

feels both amusement and annoyance. Frankie is an attorney, and she's always serious about her vocation. She's a tall, studious-looking woman with a distinctive dyke haircut and wire-rimmed eyeglasses. Despite her serious appearance, Frankie's fine-boned face gives her a special beauty, and Valerie adores her. Frankie has clear ivory skin and nipples like hard raspberries. Valerie adores serious women with fine faces and steady eyes. They've been lovers for two years and living together almost since the beginning, living together like husband and wife. Valerie is the wife and she likes it.

She continues tickling the seam of Frankie's jeans, but Frankie remains apparently oblivious to it. Is the romance over? The idea the romance could be over frightens Valerie. She's twenty-five, a brunette with a pouting mouth she likes to paint a bright red, a slender but curvy body that drives the butches wild. She knows all about it. She can see the look in their eyes in the bars when they give her the once-over, that hungry dyke look that always makes her shiver. A lover once told her what it is. The contrast. A slender femme with full breasts can make certain butches crazy. But Valerie thinks it has to be more than that because she has known women who were wild over her ass. Anyway, it's nice to be pretty and have a good body. She likes the attention. But of course it isn't the most important thing in the world. What is really important is a permanent relationship, a home, mutual giving. What is really important is peace of mind. The trouble is that even after living with Frankie two years not a day passes when Valerie isn't needy, as needy as a bitch-dog in heat, pussy-dripping needy. If not every day, then every other day. Without fail. She expected Frankie to take care of that part of her life.

Frankie takes care of her financially, but that isn't enough for Valerie. It's fine that Frankie earns enough in her law practice to give them an easy life, but Valerie thinks Frankie ought to have more consideration for the physical side. Is that asking for too much? Isn't it ridiculous to be lying here tickling Frankie's crotch without any response from Frankie? Valerie watches the images on the television tube. A woman in a red bandanna now has her mouth going, talking without stopping, saying nothing about god knows what. All I want is affection, Valerie thinks. No, it's more than that. If all she wants is affection, she'll buy a toy poodle. What she wants is good sex, the same marvelous hot sex she knows other women have. She wants Frankie to make her shake and moan until her bones are rattled. How can a woman have peace of mind without sexual fulfillment? No, it isn't possible. When she's like this, she's always so incredibly restless; no peace of mind at all. No peace of mind, Valerie thinks. With Frankie these days she never has it. She tries, though. She has no problem with Frankie when Frankie is interested. The problem is it never happens often enough—at least not enough to keep the demons out of Valerie's mind and her pussy happy. Frankie cares a great deal about her law practice, but she seems to care very little about the needy state of Valerie's poor little cunt. Twice a week on Wednesdays and Saturdays is just not enough to keep Valerie happy, to give her that look of happiness and completion that she sees on the faces of some of her friends. She's a wife, isn't she? The arrangement is that she's the wife; and if she's the wife, she thinks Frankie ought to take care of her needs.

She tickles Frankie's crotch again, determined to get Frankie interested in something beside her paperwork. She can feel the bulge of Frankie's cunt right through the fabric of Frankie's jeans. But no heat in there. She's had enough experience with Frankie to know from the feel of her crotch what state she's in. At the moment, Frankie is far away somewhere, much too far away to be interested in anything sexual. Valerie tells herself maybe she ought to wait for another time, when suddenly Frankie moves the papers away from her face and she looks down at Valerie's hand.

"What's going on?" Frankie says. "Is today Wednesday?" Valerie groans. "It's Tuesday. It's been Tuesday all day.

You don't mind if I just lie here, do you? If it bothers you, I'll stop." And then Valerie adds with a sarcastic smirk, "I wouldn't want to interfere with your work."

In a calm voice, Frankie says, "It's my work that supports us."

In a moment Frankie, returns the papers to the front of her face. Valerie now assumes she has permission to continue doing what she's been doing. but she feels foolish about it. Here she is making a blatant effort to get Frankie interested in her, and all Frankie cares about is her damn paperwork. Determined not to give up, Valerie now rolls over to face Frankie's crotch.

Frankie groans. "Val, honey...."

"Just keep doing what you're doing. Pay no attention to me."

"That's hardly possible."

"Try it." Valerie pulls at the zipper of Frankie's fly. The jeans are tight, but not tight enough to prevent her fingers from getting in there. She feels the crinkly bush through the panties, and then she strokes farther down to the soft folds of Frankie's cunt.

Valerie says, "Let me get the jeans off." And

Frankie rustles her papers and groans again. "Oh, Val."

"Frankie, please...."

Valerie hates begging Frankie like this, but there seems to be no alternative. She rolls off the sofa to get Frankie's jeans off her legs, and then she stretches out again with her head in Frankie's lap and her excitement more intense than ever as she faces Frankie's panty-covered cunt.

In the beginning, when they first started living together, most of the sex consisted of Valerie remaining passive while Frankie took the lead in starting things and carrying things through and finishing things. In the beginning, Frankie seemed to have only one objective in her mind, and that was to make certain Valerie had the most pleasure possible out of every sexual encounter between them.

Valerie isn't certain precisely when things changed, but after they were together a year, she knew the sexual part of their relationship was no longer the same. Gradually it was no longer Frankie who initiated sex, it was Valerie; until finally one day Frankie said she needed her time to be more predictable, so maybe they ought to agree to Wednesday and Saturday nights. "We'll make Wednesday and Saturday nights just for us," Frankie said, which appealed to Valerie because at least she'd have those two nights with Frankie without Frankie ever complaining. The trouble was that two nights were just not enough for Valerie, and before long she realized it and the two nights a week supposedly only for them became an agony for her whenever she wanted sex and it was neither Wednesday nor Saturday. It isn't that Frankie is that rigid about the calendar—she isn't, but it's always up to Valerie to make the move and take the chance that Frankie will reject her and

11

leave her depressed, or even worse they'll have an argument about something trivial to hide the incongruence of their sexual attitudes.

Valerie now carefully tugs the crotch of Frankie's panties aside to expose the full lips of Frankie's cunt. Not much hair on the lips. More of it on the mound. Frankie has her papers in front of her face again, and Valerie has no idea what Frankie's response might be. She's afraid Frankie might stop her, but instead Frankie merely squirms a bit on the cushion without closing her thighs. Valerie tells herself, thank God, maybe something will happen after all.

She has always adored Frankie's cunt. Frankie's clitoris is a luscious little knob just visible at the apex of the outer lips. Valerie thinks maybe later, when Frankie is aroused enough, she'll suck it, lick it with the flat of her tongue like an ice cream cone, then give it a tongue whipping. But at the moment she intends to excite Frankie with her fingers first because Frankie has strange inhibitions about cunnilingus. Frankie likes doing it to Valerie, but whenever Valerie does it to Frankie, Frankie seems embarrassed. Which Valerie thinks is so sad. Next to being totally possessed by a woman's fingers and mouth, what Valerie likes most is licking and sucking a lover's cunt. How sad it is that Frankie has problems with it.

Using the tips of her fingers, Valerie carefully strokes the folds of Frankie's cunt until the outer lips part to reveal more of the inside. Hardly any wetness. Just a hint of moisture lower down where the vaginal opening gapes slightly because Frankie once had a child that died in infancy. Something never discussed. Never mentioned. But always in the mind of Valerie whenever she looks closely at Frankie's cunt. She looks at the opening and she thinks how wondrous it is that a child came out of there. Miracles.

She has an urge to suck Frankie now. Or at least to lick her everywhere. Make her moan. It might work, but Frankie might also get angry. Valerie wonders why in hell she ever agreed to live with a woman—marry a woman—whose interest in sex is less than her own.

No, not yet, she thinks. She won't give up the ghost yet. She tugs the crotch of Frankie's panties back into place and she rises from Frankie's lap. "I'll be right back," Valerie says.

Frankie rustles her papers and mumbles something, as if she assumes Valerie is merely off to the bathroom.

But Valerie has something else in mind. When she reaches the bedroom, it isn't the adjoining bathroom she wants, but one of the drawers in the large bureau they share. Frankie has half the drawers, Valerie has the others. From one of her own drawers, Valerie pulls out a black lace garter belt and a pair of sheer charcoal stockings. Skimpy feminine lace and nylon. Never mind the politics—Valerie doesn't give a damn about lesbian politics. She believes nothing can be wrong with doing something if it turns her on or turns on her lover. Never mind the pompous dykes who think they know what every woman needs. She has enticed Frankie with these items often enough to know they can work. That was especially true in the beginning of their romance when Frankie was less constrained about playing games during sex, less inhibited about Valerie dressing up to excite them both with the accoutrements of feminine availability. These days Frankie is more political, and she often seems embarrassed by the feminine trappings, as if she indeed thinks sexy lingerie is out of place in a true lesbian relationship. A notion that Valerie thinks ridiculous. Who the hell can identify a true lesbian relationship? But she never debates with Frankie

13

because Frankie, after all, is a lawyer. Only idiots debate with lawyers.

Valerie hopes the frills might work tonight. She strips her clothes off quickly and studies herself in the full-length mirror attached to the bathroom door. Still attractive, isn't she? Still young enough to look good from any angle. Five-eight is a good height. As long as she keeps her weight down, her body looks slender and trim. She runs her fingers over the undersides of her full breasts. Watching herself in the mirror. Jiggling the firm globes and smiling at the way the tips vibrate. Unable to resist the urge to use her mouth, she raises her right breast with her hand and she swabs her tongue over the long nipple, wetting it down, then taking the nipple between her teeth to suck on it briefly. God, she needs something tonight! She runs her hands over her hips and back to the firm flesh of her buttocks. She tells herself Frankie is a fool not to appreciate her more. There are women out there who would do plenty. She slides her fingers into the curls of the dark muff beneath her belly. Her pubic triangle is thick enough to completely hide her labia. She remembers a woman she knew who shaved everything, the lips clean and silky and exposed. On occasion Valerie trims some of the hair away to show more of herself, but she's a brunette, and she doubts her dark lips would look better without hair. Still, it might be worth trying sometime just to amuse herself. Maybe shock Frankie, who isn't that experienced. Would Frankie be shocked? As far as Valerie knows, she's Frankie's first serious lover. But Frankie hardly ever talks about the other women she has known.

Now Valerie touches herself again, aware of her wet pussy, the juice trickling between her thighs, the fountain flowing the way it always does when she's this turned on. But she resists the urge to stroke herself. She turns to the garter belt and stockings, sits down on the edge of the bed, and starts pulling on the stockings. Making her legs sleek. And exciting herself doing it. By the time she finishes hooking the stockings to the garter belt, her pussy is wetter than ever. She brings a pair of heels out of the closet—sexy red pumps she hasn't worn in ages. She slips her feet into them, looks at her legs in the sheer charcoal stockings, her sleek legs, then searches the closet again to find the black negligée Frankie bought her shortly after they became lovers. Valerie remembers now how embarrassed Frankie seemed giving her the negligée, Frankie blushing when Valerie pulled the fluffy thing out of the box and squealed with joy that she loved negligées. Happy she could wear one and look good in it. Now slipping into the black negligée. She ties the front bow and then she does a whirl in front of the full length mirror to see the effect. After that she puts some fresh lipstick on her lips, bright red, not too much because Frankie never likes her to overdo it. Valerie tells herself she'll cry if this doesn't work. She will truly cry if this fails to get Frankie interested.

High heels clicking on the parquet floor, Valerie walks into the living room aware of how she looks; the red heels, the stockings, her dark nipples and dark bush revealed by the sheer negligée. Frankie glances up from the papers in her hands, her eyes showing immediate surprise.

"Good God, Val!"

"Just an urge to dress up," Valerie says. "You don't mind, do you? I thought you might like it." She does a turn that sends the negligée swirling around her nylon-clad legs. "Do you like my legs?"

"You know I like your legs." Frankie's eyes take in the legs and the high heels and the negligée and she seems flustered. "You look fabulous, but I do need to read these briefs. And it's not Wednesday, you know."

"I won't bother you, Frankie. I promise."

"Honey, I can't work while you're parading around like that. Just give me an hour, okay? I'll see you in an hour in the bedroom."

Crushed, Valerie turns and walks back to the bedroom and shuts the door. What I need is a lover, she thinks, someone outside the relationship she has with Frankie, someone outside her marriage to Frankie. Her crumbling marriage. Because that's what it is, isn't it? She loves Frankie and she can't imagine not living with her, but she just can't go on like this. She never imagined she'd ever want any woman but Frankie, but getting a lover seems the only way to keep her sanity.

Now she slips off the negligée and studies herself in the long mirror again, looks at herself wearing the garter belt and nylons, at the erotic image of her dark cunt bush framed by black lace. Pathetic, isn't she? A whimper of frustration comes out of her throat as she realizes how aroused she is. She cups her buttocks with her hands, squeezing and pinching the firm globes. Then she moves both hands around to the front, and she pinches her cunt with her fingers. She moans softly as she feels how wet she is. She starts gyrating her hips in front of the mirror, her eyes fixed on her hairy cunt. Ever so slowly, she pulls her thick labia open with her fingers to reveal the quivering pearl of her clit. Oh God, look at it—look how swollen it is. One touch and she'll come immediately. Instead, she moves her hands away, her palms sliding over her body to keep the tension rising. Thank God she knows how to pleasure herself when she needs it. She'd surely go crazy without it. Just the hole, she thinks. If she keeps her fingers away from her clit, she can play with her cunt and delay things as long as she wants. She always needs something in there. She slips her fingers down, probes around the vaginal entrance, stretches it a bit, then pushes her fingers inside and jerks her pelvis forward because it feels so good.

She moans. She uses her left hand to lift her right breast. Watching herself in the mirror, she lowers her head and licks the nipple until it gleams with her saliva. Both nipples are stiff and swollen. She quivers as her eyes take in the way the black straps of her garter belt frame her cunt bush. Her long legs look so sleek and lovely in the sheer charcoal stockings, her calves exquisitely flexed by the four-inch heels of the red pumps. After turning sideways, she looks over her shoulder at the shape of her ass, then cups a hand over one buttock and jiggles it. Will she ever be able to find a lover who can give her body the attention it deserves?

Now she leaves the mirror, and she falls across the bed on her back with her thighs wide open. With a soft moan, she slides her hands down over her body to the steaming flower of her cunt. She gasps and jerks, her hips arching upward as she closes her right hand over the hot mound of her pussy and slowly massages the dripping lips. How she loves the feel of her wetness beneath her fingers! Her cunt is loose and quivering now, ready to be loved and cuddled and provided with ecstasies. She spreads her throbbing labia and dips her fingers inside her vaginal opening. She groans as a delicious hot spasm washes over her body. Stretching the mouth of her cunt with a screwing motion of her fingers, she gradually slips her fingers deeper and deeper inside her canal. She can feel the muscles in there grabbing at her fingers. Her eyes closed, her mouth open, she spreads her quivering thighs wide apart as she imagines she has a lover between her legs, a woman with a hard body and a long tongue, a tongue long enough and thick enough to fill her completely, and a tongue strong enough to lap her clit as long as she needs it. Valerie shudders as she starts stabbing her fingers in and out, twisting them enough to stretch the tissues around her clit and bring her closer and closer to an intense orgasm. Waves of pleasure engulf her senses. She bucks her hips, fucking back at her pumping hand, her fingers making a wet sound each time they plunge inward.

Suddenly the bedroom door opens, Frankie steps into the room and then freezes as she takes in the scene.

Valerie cries out, jerks her hand away from her crotch and rolls over onto her belly with a groan. "Frankie, why don't you knock?"

Frankie's voice has an icy calm. "It's my bedroom too, Val."

Valerie sighs into the pillow. "Yes, I guess so. I guess it's my fault."

Silence. Frankie says nothing, but Valerie can feel Frankie's eyes staring at her. Then Valerie hears Frankie pass the bed, and the next moment she hears Frankie walk into the bathroom and close the door.

Valerie lies there listening, her heart beating wildly, wondering what will happen now. She knows how much Frankie hates the idea of secret masturbation. Never in secret, Frankie told her. If we need that, we ought to be able to help each other. Valerie hears the sound of the toilet flushing. Then, a few moments later, she hears Frankie brushing her teeth.

The bathroom door opens and Frankie says, "Val?"

"Yes?"

"Let's wait until tomorrow, okay? I'm just too

tired this evening, too preoccupied with some things at the office. You don't mind, do you, honey? Tomorrow's Wednesday, and we'll have a lovely time together."

A cold chill passes up Valerie's spine. "Sure, Frankie, whatever you want."

When Frankie closes the bathroom door again, Valerie rolls over on her back and moves a hand down to her cunt. She has to finish what she started now. Frankie as much as told her to do that. Valerie quickly slips her fingers inside her cunt and she begins fucking herself. The orgasm arrives within moments, her juices drenching her pumping hand as she continues jerking her wrist.

I can't go on, she thinks. She'll get a lover. No matter what, she'll get a lover because she can't go on this way. Oh, no.

Rising at last, she wipes her hand on the bed sheet, and she begins unhooking the stockings to get ready for bed. By the time Frankie comes out of the bathroom, Valerie is under the covers with her back turned, her eyes closed. Valerie feels a great relief when Frankie slides into bed and does no more than kiss her shoulder before rolling away to sleep.

The darkness is a refuge.

# TWO

# Frankie

Frankie notices the girl as soon as she enters the elevator. The two of them are alone together, Frankie just returning from a boring lunch with a pair of LaSalle Street attorneys, and now here is this interesting girl riding up with her in the elevator. More a woman than girl, maybe twenty-four or twenty-five, a chunky brunette with big breasts under a tight sweater, and a manner of looking at Frankie that says they have something in common. Recognition. Whenever it happens this way, unexpected, Frankie is always thrilled because it means there are so many women out there unknown to her who might be available. She does have Valerie, but Valerie is domestic and this is foreign—an unknown girl—and unknown girls are always exciting.

Frankie starts the conversation, mentioning something about the weather, and then about the building and the air conditioning and how sometimes it's too warm in the office, all the while her eyes taking in the girl's tight sweater, the big breasts, wondering what the nipples are like. "Aren't you warm in that sweater?"

The girl gives her a wry smile. "No, it's not too heavy." But the breasts are heavy. Oh, my, yes. Frankie can tell that the girl is wearing a bra, full support for those lovely tits.

They talk some more, Frankie learning the girl is visiting a dentist on her floor and, as they step out of the elevator, Frankie makes a joke about how awful it is to have a frozen anesthetized mouth after a visit to the dentist.

"Oh, I'm just having a cleaning," the girl says.

"I'm due for one myself," Frankie says. "But I've been so busy in court, there's no time."

"You're a lawyer?" A look that says the girl is impressed.

"That's right."

They have now stopped in front of Frankie's office, the girl hesitating a moment before she says, "Gee, I could use a lawyer, I'm having so much trouble with my landlord."

Frankie chuckles. "Well, here I am. But you've got that dental appointment now, don't you? Maybe we could meet for a drink later on."

"Sure, I'd love that." "There's a place called Ricky's just around the corner. How about four o'clock?"

So easy. Before they say good-by, Frankie learns that the girl is a nurse and her name is Marcia. Which makes Frankie more excited than ever, because the one thing she knows for certain is that nurses can be hot.

24

Ricky's is crowded, the usual late-afternoon gaggle of executive types pretending to foster business connections. Frankie takes a seat at the long bar, orders a whiskey sour, and waits. Promptly at five minutes past four, Marcia arrives and sits down next to her with a smile. "Well, I'm here."

Frankie asks her what she's drinking and then buys her a daiquiri. "I haven't been in here in ages," Frankie says.

Marcia chuckles and leans closer. "Listen, I just want to be sure we're on the same track."

"What track is that?"

"Do you read *Gay News*?"

"I do sometimes."

"I'm just trying to make sure about you. Anyway, I'm living with someone, and I want you to know that."

"So am I." Marcia laughs again and says her lover is out of town. "She's in Los Angeles until next Tuesday."

"And mine's right at home." Marcia raises her glass. "Well, here's to home sweet home."

"And to us."

"Sure, why not?"

Frankie feels happy as she gazes at the front of Marcia's sweater. "Do you mind if I say something dirty?"

Marcia giggles. "Hurry up and tell me."

"I'd like to get you in a corner and fuck you silly."

Marcia flushes and giggles again. "Come on, there's no one at my place, so why are we sitting here?"

Why indeed? They kiss in the taxi, Marcia leaning against Frankie to accept a tender kiss on her cheek, both afraid to do more because the cabdriver keeps talking about the traffic, the government, the holes in the streets. When they finally arrive in front of the building where Marcia lives, they hurry out of the taxi and into the cluttered apartment. More kissing as soon as the door is closed. Now Frankie can get a hand on Marcia's breasts, feeling the curves, the weight of them. Marcia moans as she sucks on Frankie's probing tongue. Frankie drops her hand down to get it under Marcia's skirt, between her thighs, and into the wet crotch of her pantyhose. "Oh, Jesus, I'm hot," Marcia says. Frankie kisses her and rubs her cunt through her pantyhose at the same time, keeps rubbing until Marcia groans against her mouth and comes. After that they kiss some more, sweaty frenzied kissing in the hallway just inside the front door of the apartment. Marcia has her turn with Frankie, her hand sliding under Frankie's gray wool skirt to clutch at Frankie's cunt, squeeze the lips and jerk her fingers against her clit and coax her. "Come on, baby." And Frankie shudders, humping her cunt at Marcia's hand, both of them awash with sweat and juice and the frenzy of a new fuck.

They finally disentangle themselves, but they walk into the bedroom with their arms around each other's waists. Marcia apologizes for the mess in the bedroom, the clothes and underwear draped over the chairs and doorknobs. "I wasn't expecting company. Don't look."

"You're the only thing I'm looking at."

Marcia gives her a coquettish glance as she starts undressing. "I sure didn't think anything interesting would happen to me today. Not on the way to the dentist, anyhow."

Frankie has her jacket off, her fingers unbuttoning her blouse as she watches Marcia pull her sweater over her head. And there they are, Marcia's luscious breasts packed into that simple white bra like a pair of melons waiting to be tasted. Marcia knows her own assets, and in a moment she has the bra unhooked and pulled away from her body to show herself.

"That's better," Marcia says. She laughs as she holds her big breasts with her hands. "I saw you looking at these in the elevator when we first met. You were looking, weren't you?"

"Yes, I was."

"Eating up my tits with your eyes." Frankie has to have them, and she stops undressing and she walks over to get her face between the two lovely breasts. She takes one of the fat nipples in her mouth, sucking at it, whipping it with her tongue as Marcia groans with pleasure. Then Marcia pulls Frankie's head up and they kiss again, Marcia's naked breasts pushing against Frankie's blouse. They press against each other, their breasts and bellies rubbing, Frankie's knee sliding up between Marcia's thighs to massage her crotch.

Marcia giggles. "Hey, let's get our clothes off while there's a bed here."

When they separate, Marcia quickly drops her skirt. As she bends over to retrieve it, her breasts swing from side to side like a pair of white honeydews. Now all she wears is the sheer black pantyhose with a lace panty, her solid legs and thighs gleaming through the nylon, a generous dark bush visible through the lace in the crotch. With a coy look at Frankie, she walks over to the dressing table, picks up a hairbrush, and starts brushing her hair.

"You're slow," Marcia says.

"I'm busy looking at you."

"I could lose ten pounds, but every time I try, I gain it back."

"Never mind, you're perfect."

"You're not so bad yourself, but I wish I could see more."

But instead of waiting for Frankie to undress, Marcia now puts down the hairbrush and peels off her pantyhose. Since she has her back partly turned toward Frankie, it's her ass that Frankie fixes her eyes on, Marcia's luscious full buttocks with a cleft so deep Frankie has an urge to bury her face in it.

Naked, Marcia climbs onto the bed and lies on her side facing Frankie. Her rosy skin catches the light of the lamp on the night table. She has a thick pubic bush, a mass of dark curled hair at the joining of her thighs. As if to tease Frankie, she keeps her legs closed to hide her cunt.

Frankie finishes undressing while Marcia watches her with bright eyes. All Frankie can think about is Marcia's breasts, those lovely brown nipples. She hungers to have Marcia's breasts in her mouth.

When Frankie is naked, Marcia says, "You look great, like a runner. Do you do any of that?"

Frankie nods, proud of her athletic body. "I run when I can, usually on weekends." She's happy that Marcia likes her body. Sometimes she thinks that Valerie takes it for granted. Frankie is convinced Valerie is a great narcissist, always loving her own body more than someone else's.

Now Frankie climbs onto the bed and she moves forward to take Marcia in her arms. They kiss, their mouths fusing, their tongues wagging against each other.

Marcia moans. "I really like you."

"And I like you, too."

"You know, sometimes you meet someone, and it just doesn't work. This is working, isn't it?"

"Yes, it is." They kiss again. Frankie slides a hand down to Marcia's cunt to explore her thicket of pubic hair. Marcia opens her legs, making herself available, her thick-lipped pussy dripping on Frankie's probing fingers. A smell of woman-heat fills Frankie's nostrils, making her mind whirl with excitement. She rubs her open palm over Marcia's hairy cunt, thrilled by the wet feel of it. Then she parts the lush lips and slowly pushes two fingers inside the opening. Marcia groans as Frankie takes her, her elastic canal gripping Frankie's fingers as Frankie begins a slow stroking in and out of her vagina. When Frankie uses another finger to tickle Marcia's anus, Marcia cries out and starts coming immediately. "Oh, God, yes, do it!"

Frankie's pleasure lies in watching her come. Marcia's face glistens with sweat. Her mouth hangs open, her eyes are closed. As Frankie's fingers continue stroking in and out of her vagina, Marcia makes whimpering sounds in her throat and sometimes bites her lower lip. She begs for more, hunching at Frankie's hand. Frankie makes her open her legs wide, and then she begins a hard fucking with her fingers that makes Marcia cry out with pleasure. Frankie delights in making Marcia come again and again. Her hand wet with Marcia's juices, Frankie urges her on. "Don't stop, sweet. Keep coming." Marcia tosses on the bed, her ass heaving, her sopping cunt slamming against Frankie's invading fingers. At the end, she rolls over on her back with her knees in the air while Frankie kneels in front of her, driving her fingers in and out like a battering ram.

When Marcia comes down, she groans. "Oh, Jesus, you're good."

Her fingers out of Marcia's vagina but still stroking her thighs, Frankie chuckles. "No, it's not me, it's you." And then she slides her fingers down farther to touch the puckered ring of Marcia's anus.

Marcia smiles and pulls her knees up again. "You could be a nurse. Nurses like to get their fingers everywhere."

Frankie blushes and pulls her fingers away, but Marcia laughs as she tugs Frankie's hand back to her ass. "No, go on, I like it. I can come that way. But slide up a little so I can touch you. Do it to me in both holes."

Both holes. The words make Frankie quiver. She's always inhibited by assplay, but she finds it exciting because it's nasty. She hardly ever does it with Valerie, even if sometimes she thinks that Valerie wants it. Some things you don't do with the person closest to you. With Marcia there is no need to wonder whether she wants; it's obvious she does. After lubricating her fingers in Marcia's cunt, Frankie finds she can easily slide two fingers inside Marcia's anus. The chunky brunette groans as she takes the fingers, and then she wants something in her cunt and Frankie uses her thumb there.

"Oh, that's great," Marcia says with a gasp.

"I'm afraid I'll hurt you."

Marcia giggles. "Don't worry about that. I'm a nurse. I know what I'm doing."

Meanwhile Marcia has managed to get a hand between Frankie's thighs, and her fingers are now hooked inside Frankie's wet cunt, holding onto Frankie as Frankie starts fucking Marcia with her hand. Frankie's excitement is intense. Marcia pushes her fingers deep inside Frankie's cunt and groans as Frankie's fingers move in both openings. Frankie loves getting dirty like this with a new girl. The fact that Marcia is a nurse excites her. She keeps her fingers moving slowly, driving her thumb inside Marcia's cunt to the last knuckle each time she pushes her hand forward. Marcia starts coming and it seems endless, her body shaking, the cries coming out of her throat as Frankie keeps her hand moving. At the end, Frankie bends over to take one of Marcia's fat nipples in her mouth. She sucks and bites the nipple, the biting making Marcia come again.

"Oh, hell, don't stop!" Marcia says, grabbing Frankie's wrist as Frankie is about to pull her fingers out.

Frankie is amused. "Are you sure?"

"Just a little more."

So Frankie gives Marcia what she wants, a little more in both openings, at the same time humping her cunt at Marcia's hand. Marcia says she loves assfucking, and she never gets enough of it. Frankie's cunt is hot and dripping, her clit swollen. She comes suddenly, jerking her pussy at Marcia's fingers, feeling her juices running everywhere.

They kiss after that, Marcia's ass gripping Frankie's fingers as Frankie slowly pulls them out of both openings. Marcia giggles and says Frankie is as good as her lover the way she does her ass. Frankie is a bit embarrassed talking about it, but she likes looking at Marcia's luscious ass when Marcia rolls over onto her belly.

After that Frankie excuses herself and she goes to the bathroom still excited by the sex, her hands trembling as she washes them. She uses a towel to wipe her cunt and the insides of her thighs, and then she studies her face in the mirror, her flushed cheeks. She always looks good after sex. She thinks about Marcia and Marcia's hot body, and then she thinks about getting home to another dull evening with Valerie. Oh, hell, Frankie thinks.

# THREE

# Valerie

As Valerie expects, she and Frankie do make love Wednesday evening. After dinner Frankie comes up behind her in the kitchen and says, "Let's do something." She takes Valerie into the bedroom, undresses her, makes her lie down on the bed, and then fucks her with her fingers. After the first orgasm, Frankie says, "Are you all right?"

"Come on top of me," Valerie says. And Frankie does that. She peels off her jeans and underpants and she climbs into the saddle to fuck Valerie again, this time with her cunt. Valerie likes it because she has the pleasure of holding Frankie's buttocks in her hands while Frankie humps and pummels her pussy. She comes again, crying out, her arms and legs wrapped around Frankie as if to hold her and keep her from leaving her.

But Frankie is now exhausted, and she says so as

she pulls away. "No more, honey, I'm drained."

"Let me suck you."

"No, I'm fine. What I really want now is a hot bath and some wine. Will you get the wine for me?"

Valerie brings Frankie the wine in her bath, and then Valerie closes the bathroom door and leaves her alone. In the kitchen, Valerie wonders if she ought to have some wine, too. No, she doesn't want wine, she wants a lover.

She wants a lover, but she also wants no trouble with Frankie. She's afraid to go to one of the bars because too many people know about them—know them as a couple—which means too much of a risk that Frankie will learn about it. But there seems no other way to meet anyone. She will not go to a lesbian group because she never connects well with political lesbians. No, there is no way except a bar. She decides to try it first in the afternoon. She'll feel safer in daylight. If she meets anyone she knows, she can pretend she's interested in nothing more than getting out of the sun and cooling off with a beer.

And so a few days later Valerie goes to a place called Augie's. It's mid-afternoon, but inside the bar it's dark, the air cool and the music heavily erotic. Valerie is relieved when a quick glance around the room reveals no one she knows, none of Frankie's friends and none of her own. She sits alone at the bar, and by the time she is on her second beer, she feels more at ease and happy she has finally decided to be adventurous.

Someone finally approaches her, comes up behind her and says, "Like some company?"

The woman's voice is smooth and self-assured, and when Valerie turns to look at her, she likes her immediately. Valerie noticed her before, a rangy-looking butch with wide shoulders in a white shirt, jeans and cowboy boots, graying blond hair slicked back and cool blue eyes.

"I don't mind," Valerie says. The woman says her name is Cleo. She sits on a stool beside Valerie and orders two beers for them.

"Nothing like a cold beer on a hot afternoon," Cleo says, giving Valerie's breasts an approving glance before lifting her eyes to smile at her.

Valerie nods, already feeling the first twitches of excitement in her belly. "Yes, a cold beer is nice."

They start talking. Cleo asks whether Valerie has a lover and Valerie says yes, but things aren't working out that well. Cleo says she and her lover split a few weeks ago. "Makes me lonely," Cleo says. Then Cleo looks closely at Valerie. "You're not straight, are you? I don't get along well with straight girls."

Valerie blushes, wondering whether a straight woman would ever wander into a place like Augie's. "No, I'm living with a woman."

Cleo chuckles. "That's better." They make small talk for fifteen minutes or so. Before long, Cleo's arm is around Valerie's waist and Cleo's knee is pressing against Valerie's with a firmness that heightens Valerie's excitement. Valerie pretends she's in the bar merely to cool off, and for a while Cleo plays along with her and says nothing suggestive. Valerie's mind, however, is filled with erotic images of Cleo doing things to her, Cleo fondling and caressing her, sucking her nipples, kissing her belly, dropping her mouth between her legs and licking her cunt until she goes crazy. She imagines Cleo's long fingers inside her. She imagines Cleo's cunt pushing against her mouth as Cleo fucks her face. After another fifteen minutes, Valerie catches herself trembling with anticipation. Cleo seems to sense it and makes her move, strokes

Valerie's back, and says her place isn't far and maybe they ought to go there because they'll be more comfortable. If Valerie likes jazz, they can listen to Cleo's tapes. Valerie agrees, but of course she doesn't care about the jazz, and neither does Cleo. They both know they're going to Cleo's place to fuck. Swaying a bit after four beers, Valerie waltzes out of Augie's on Cleo's arm and feels happy that Cleo hails a taxi.

"Better than walking," Cleo says, helping Valerie into the cab and then sliding in beside her and giving the driver the address. As soon as the taxi starts moving, Cleo leans against Valerie and licks Valerie's ear. "You're beautiful," Cleo says.

Valerie shudders and turns her face to be kissed. As their mouths fuse, Cleo's hand slides under the edge of Valerie's dress to stroke Valerie's knees. Valerie is wearing heels, but her legs are bare. The feel of Cleo's fingers tickling her knees and thighs makes her shiver with excitement.

When they finish kissing, Cleo keeps her head against Valerie's and says, "I'm crazy about your legs. That's the first thing I noticed when you walked in. I like legs in heels."

Valerie quivers. "I can't stay more than a few hours."

"I promise not to tie you down."

Valerie giggles. "I bet you do that, too."

"Only on request."

"Well, I'm not requesting it, so don't think of it."

"All right, I'll think of other things." And the way she looks at Valerie makes it clear that whatever she's thinking about is hot and exciting.

The taxi finally arrives at Cleo's place. Cleo pays the driver and they climb out. Cleo's apartment is tidy and comfortably furnished. She tells Valerie she runs a truck-rental agency and is doing well at it.

"How about some vodka?" Cleo says. Valerie says yes, accepts a vodka tonic, hoping Cleo won't dawdle too long because she's too nervous. But instead of dawdling, Cleo soon moves quickly, and within a few minutes after the drinks are poured in the living room, Valerie is in Cleo's arms.

"I bet you're a hot girl," Cleo says, her voice husky against Valerie's ear. The older woman drops her big hands down to squeeze Valerie's buttocks through her skirt. "Nice, doll. I like the way you're put together." Then Cleo chuckles. "Am I coming on too strong for you? Just tell me if I am. I don't want any bad vibrations getting started."

One hand holding onto Cleo's strong shoulder, Valerie sips her drink and says, "I think I'm doing fine."

Cleo laughs. "Good girl." Valerie crosses her arms behind Cleo's head as they stand there and kiss. A spine-melting thrill passes through Valerie as she feels Cleo's hand drop to the small of her back to press their bellies together more firmly. Cleo grinds her hips against Valerie's as she whispers in Valerie's ear that Valerie has her steaming. "You're a doll," Cleo says.

Happy, Valerie rubs her belly against Cleo's to let her know she wants more. Cleo's hands slide over Valerie's shoulders and down her arms to her waist. Cleo's lips trail over Valerie's throat, then down to the low neckline of her dress. The older woman's fingers graze over Valerie's breasts, then settle on Valerie's right breast to play with the nipple through Valerie's blouse and bra. Valerie shudders. She goes limp as Cleo's fingers squeeze the nipple, pull and tug at it. She moans as she feels the buzzing connection between her breasts and cunt. When she squeezes her thighs together, she can feel the wetness between her legs.

She loves it. Frankie never makes her feel like this, certainly hasn't for a long time. Cleo seems to know how to turn a woman on, how to get the furnace fired up and blazing.

Cleo undresses her while they're standing, unbuttons her blouse, unzips her skirt, strips her down to bra and panties, and then makes her sit on the sofa. Dropping down to her knees, the rangy blonde starts kissing Valerie's legs and thighs and then finally buries her face in Valerie's crotch.

Valerie groans and lifts her knees. High heels wagging in the air, she looks down to watch Cleo sniffing her cunt through her panties, sniffing at the crotch already soaked with juice, nuzzling it, teasing her by not removing her panties. Not even her bra is off yet, the bra she likes to wear only because her breasts need support. She wants Cleo to remove her bra, but Cleo is too busy between her legs, busy driving her crazy with her hot breath blowing against her panty-covered cunt. Suddenly, with a low sound in her throat, Cleo clamps her mouth over Valerie's cunt and begins chewing the swollen lips through her panties.

Valerie moans and closes her eyes. She remembers how Frankie once did this when they first started dating. A hot date dancing in a bar. Then a run to Frankie's place, where she had Valerie on the sofa with her dress up. Frankie's face buried in Valerie's sopping crotch. Valerie was drunk enough to hunch wildly, scream, lift her pelvis, begging Frankie to get her pantyhose off and fuck her. Valerie remembered the hot look in Frankie's eyes as she started chewing the nylon instead, eating her through her pantyhose, eating her all the way to a fantastic orgasm that made her scream.

Cleo is eating her now, sucking her through the

panties to make her crotch a soggy mess of saliva and juice, eating her pussy with such incredible energy. Wanting her. Valerie tells herself this is what she needs. To be wanted like this. She keeps her legs up, her knees back, the high heels pointed at the ceiling. She remembers Cleo telling her earlier that she likes legs in heels. Now Cleo's face and hair graze the insides of her thighs. Cleo's long fingers clutch at her ass through the panties. Cleo's face is wet. Valerie can see the wetness on Cleo's face when she looks down at her. Frankie never shows the wet on her face. Frankie always makes sure to wipe it off before she comes up again. Valerie has never been kissed by Frankie with a wet mouth, never tasted herself on Frankie's lips. Her own taste. Never had Frankie suck her through her panties with such force. She spreads her legs wider now, her legs straight out and wide open, offering Cleo everything she has.

Then Cleo pulls her face away and she wipes her mouth with the back of her hand. Without awkwardness. "You're hot, aren't you, doll?"

Valerie quivers, her legs still up and apart. "Can't you tell?"

Cleo laughs. "I'm just teasing you." One of her fingers slides under the edge of Valerie's panties to touch a lip. "Dripping," Cleo says. "You're dripping right through your pants."

Valerie moans. "Don't tease!"

"I ought to tie you up and really tease you."

"No, please...."

Groaning, squirming her ass with frustration as Cleo goes down again. Cleo's tongue laps over the outside of Valerie's panties. Valerie has an urge to tear a hole in the panties to get that tongue inside her.

Then, at last, Cleo pulls away. No more. She gently

urges Valerie's legs down, and she chuckles. "Enough, doll. Let's get to the bedroom and have some comfort."

She takes Valerie's hand, helps her rise, leads her out of the living room.

Now you belong to her, Valerie thinks. At least for a while, anyway. Wearing only her bra and panties while Cleo is still fully dressed. She feels slutty. But the feeling is wonderful, her body keyed up to a high pitch of anticipation.

In the bedroom, she stretches out on the bed. Cleo climbs on and begins kissing her again, more slowly, a romantic pecking, kissing and licking her mouth, then fluttering her tongue down between her breasts, over her rib cage and into her navel. At last Cleo rises to undress, her eyes hot. Valerie watches the clothes come off. When Cleo strips her shirt off, there is no bra to hide her breasts. She has small breasts on a lanky body, more lanky than Frankie. But the nipples are pink, instead of brown like Frankie's. When Cleo is down to her underpants, Valerie can see the wetness in her crotch, her juices seeping through the cotton, the evidence she wants Valerie. Evidence not before the court, Valerie thinks. Stolen evidence. She feels a deep pleasure at the sight of another woman responding to her. Someone besides Frankie responding to her. Although she can't remember the last time she saw Frankie wetting her pants for her.

Cleo teases Valerie by pulling down her underpants very slowly. Pubic hair first. Then more of the mound. Curled blonde hair. And finally the split between the plump blonde lips as she lifts one leg to get the panties free. "Want to look?" Cleo says. Laughing, she comes to the bed, puts one foot on the edge and swings her knee wide to show everything, the pink flower open, pink flaps like wattles. She pulls at her cunt with her fingers to make her clit stick out. She's not that butch, is she? Valerie doesn't mind it, but as she looks at Cleo's cunt she thinks it's a bit silly, too blatant. But hot. A tall skinny butch with graying blonde hair and a meaty cunt. Pink cunt and those pink nipples.

Cleo looks ready for fucking, the wattles out, the slit wet. "Watch me," Cleo says. And Valerie is shocked as Cleo pushes two fingers inside herself and starts masturbating. No shyness. Her fingers slide in and out of her pink cunt. Cleo's crotch is so close, Valerie can hear the sucking sound as the fingers move in and out. And she can see the bit of flab on the insides of Cleo's thighs. And that swollen clit above the fingers jerking around like that. Cleo's thumb finds her clit and presses it down, mashes it down as if to squash it into oblivion. "Christ, I'm coming!" Cleo says, her eyes rolling up, her pelvis punching back and forth as she keeps her fingers moving. Valerie locks her thighs, squeezing her cunt with her thigh muscles, amazed at everything, amazed because everything happens so fast, amazed she's still wearing her underwear, amazed that a dyke who looks like such a strong butch would do this. While Cleo gushes. Gushing on her fingers. Her face flushed as she giggles, groans, pulls her fingers out and says, "Wow!" And laughs.

Quickly now, Valerie unsnaps her bra and peels off her panties. Cleo's eyes glitter as she takes in everything. "Nice tits," Cleo says. "I like big tits."

The strong butch again. Valerie smiles and says she isn't that big, but she moves her shoulders to make her breasts jiggle. To make Cleo want her more. Then Cleo comes onto the bed and kisses her, only this time they are both naked, the fresh contact of their bodies electric. Cleo palms Valerie's breasts, squeezing them, then bending her head to lick both nipples at the same time, digging her nose and mouth between Valerie's breasts and licking the soft skin. Then back to her nipples again, chewing on them, pulling Valerie's nipples with her teeth until they feel raw. "Does it hurt?" Cleo asks.

And Valerie tells her, "Almost," as she slips a hand down over Cleo's back and over the narrow hip to cup Cleo's blonde cunt. Maybe surprising Cleo by doing it. Valerie rubs the heel of her palm against the wet flaps, against Cleo's gushing flower, smearing the syrup around on the insides of Cleo's thighs. Valerie loves the electric pleasure of a wet cunt in her hand. Especially a new one. No matter how much she likes the stability of a monogamous relationship, the first touching of a new cunt is always wonderful. And the cunt of a strong butch is always something special.

Cleo whispers, "Go on, suck it."

Valerie blushes because she isn't ready for that. She wants Cleo to give first. She's afraid Cleo will do all the taking. Like some others she has known. The takers. Dykes who are too sleek. "No, not yet."

"Then get inside me and make me come." All right, she can do that. She pushes one of her fingers inside, then two fingers, then three fingers. Cleo groans, raises one knee. Cleo moves her ass, fucking back at Valerie's fingers, exciting Valerie because she comes so easily. Valerie's fingers are wet, sopping, drenched by the hot cunt. Delicious.

Cleo looks happy. "Hey, you're good." No butch remorse about having her cunt taken like that.

Cleo now makes Valerie lie back on the bed and open her legs, her knees up, her thighs wide apart to show her cunt. Cleo looks at it, a long look at Valerie's wide-open cunt. Valerie quivers because it turns her on so much. The lust in Cleo's eyes, the dyke hunger for pussy. Valerie groans as Cleo's fingers open her, spread the lips apart to expose everything. Cleo smiles. "I bet you're sweet like candy." Which makes Valerie blush no matter how corny it is. Sweet like candy. Her pussy sweet like candy. She wants Cleo's mouth. What is she waiting for? Looking at her like that as she lies with her cunt wide open. Cleo's fingers now pull at one of her lips, tugging it out as if to see how far it will stretch. Possessive. And maybe a bit sadistic. Then tickling her lower down in the crack of her ass. Valerie squirms, trying to avoid it. But Cleo insists, using her middle finger, pushing her wet middle finger inside Valerie's ass to see how open she is. Then pulling her finger out and again telling Valerie she's a hot doll. "You're a hot pussy," Cleo says. "Whoever you're living with, she's not taking care of you."

Valerie moans, aching. "Please do something...."

Cleo chuckles, tells her to take it easy. "We've got all afternoon, baby."

"No, I can't. I can't stay too long." She pushes Cleo's hands away from her cunt and she replaces them with her own, her fingers in the wet, pressing on the shaft of her clitoris.

Cleo laughs. "Come on, that's my job." Teasing her again, taking her time, making Valerie hold her lips open while she inspects the inside of her cunt. Then she has Valerie pinch out her clit, force it to protrude at the top of her slit, Cleo meanwhile with two fingers inside Valerie's vaginal opening. "You like to rush it too much," Cleo says.

"I can't stand being teased."

"Your pussy says something else, doll. Your pussy says you love it."

Yes, she does love it. She hikes her knees up farther as Cleo's fingers start fucking her. She rocks her legs, holding her knees back with her hands now, loving each thrust of Cleo's long fingers in her canal.

"That's it," Cleo says. "Come on, let me see you pop off." And pop off she does, her legs straight up in the air, her cunt going wild as Cleo's fingers slam her crotch again and again. At the end another cry as Cleo drops her head to clamp her mouth on her wet pussy, Valerie moaning as she drops her legs onto Cleo's shoulders. She humps at Cleo's mouth, taking the blonde butch's mouth, feeling Cleo sucking her insides out, coming hard, and then coming down as Cleo licks the wetness on the insides of her thighs.

Cleo wiping her mouth with her fingers, then licking Valerie's cream off her fingertips. "Have a beer?"

Valerie nods, watching Cleo as she leaves the bed and walks out of the bedroom, then reaching down to touch her cunt, feel the wetness, close the lips in an attempt to cool herself down.

Returning with two beers, Cleo says, "I gather you've got problems at home."

"Yes."

"She doesn't give you enough."

Embarrassed, Valerie closes her legs. "I'd rather not talk about it."

Cleo smiles as she pulls Valerie's legs apart. "Come on, don't hide it. Not from me." Her blue eyes bright as she gazes at Valerie's open cunt. "That's better." A moment later, she puts her beer away and she goes down on Valerie again, her lips and long tongue massaging Valerie's wet pussy. Valerie moans, no longer caring about anything except the mouth on her cunt, the hot twirling tongue thrusting inside her vagina. Not caring. Only this. A long blonde with a long tongue. Being wanted.

Shortly afterward, Valerie leaves the bed and hurries to get dressed again and leave. Cleo tries to stop her, but Valerie insists. "No, I can't."

"All right, here's my number, call me. Will you do that?"

"Yes." And she's out the door, trembling, steeped in a great wash of guilt, hoping she can find a taxi fast and get home quickly.

In the evening, the routine with Frankie is the same as usual. Frankie working out of her briefcase. Valerie lying on the sofa watching a silly TV program. And thinking about Cleo. This time she has something to think about, memories that make her quiver. Memories that make her hot again as she lies there on the sofa while Frankie works at the dining-room table with her papers. Valerie thinks of Cleo sucking her until she climaxed. She remains restless on the sofa until she goes to bed.

On Saturday evening, Frankie suggests they go out to a Chinese restaurant. Valerie is joyful, happy to be out with Frankie, who is sweet and loving as they sit facing each other in a booth. "I love you," Valerie says. And Frankie smiles at her. They touch hands while they wait for the food to arrive. This is everything Valerie wants. But no, not everything. She needs the sex, too. At home later it's understood they'll make love. Saturday night, isn't it? Frankie suggests they go right to bed and they do that. Maybe it's too early. They kiss under the covers. Frankie strokes Valerie's breasts and then she slips a hand between Valerie's legs. Too fast. Valerie wants more of a workup, but instead Frankie's fingers are already inside her, sliding in and out, Frankie's knuckle slamming her clit, pushing her into it, making her come. Unable to hold back. Valerie heaves, cries out, coming like crazy on Frankie's hand.

Frankie says, "Are you all right?"

"Yes."

Valerie slides a hand down to Frankie's cunt, but

Frankie stops her. "No, I'm fine. Really, I'm fine. I don't need anything."

And turns away. Leaving Valerie staring at the ceiling in the darkness. Why? How could she know why? After a while, Valerie leaves the bed and walks into the bathroom to use her fingers on her clit, rubbing herself as she leans against the wall. Bitterness and a long sob as she finally has an orgasm.

On Monday she telephones Cleo. "My lovely doll," Cleo says. A sultry happiness in her voice. They make a date for one o'clock the next afternoon at Cleo's place. "I'll be waiting, doll."

# FOUR

# Cleo

After Cleo puts the phone down, she walks back to the living room and she smiles at the girl on the sofa. "Are you okay, doll? Would you like another drink?"

The girl's name is Susan. She's a sandy blonde, a college girl with long, silky hair, a long body now extended on Cleo's sofa. She looks at Cleo with seductive eyes and shakes her head. "No, I'm fine, thank you."

Cleo is solicitous, affectionate, seating herself on the sofa now beside Susan's long legs. Susan wears a summer dress and sandals, and she's bare-legged. Cleo runs her hand over one of the girl's lovely legs. "You could be a model."

Susan smiles. "I'm not that pretty."

"Yes you are. You're a knockout." Cleo picked her up only a few hours ago in a bar, and now Cleo is congratulating herself because the girl is such a beauty and so obviously hungry to be fucked. The girls are always easy when they're looking for it, especially the rich college girls from Northwestern. Cleo is forty-six, happy in her maturity, happy because she's having more success with women these days than she had when she was Susan's age. At Susan's age she was a totally mixed-up Sixties flower child. Now she's a middle-aged dyke with a settled mind and uncomplicated desires. There is nothing complicated about the desire she feels for Susan. Cleo is thrilled as Susan now slowly raises one knee, the movement causing her dress to fall back enough to reveal one of her thighs. The girl knows what she's doing. Oh, yes.

Susan wears hardly any makeup, but her lips are painted a bright red. She likes to toss her long blonde hair, tossing it over one shoulder or over the other shoulder, or sometimes pulling a strand or two away from her face. Her body is long, but the curves are there, a hint of heaviness in the breasts and hips that delights Cleo. The older woman imagines those ripe breasts in her hands. That makes her think of Valerie's breasts, Valerie's voice on the phone just a few minutes ago, Valerie's dark-haired muff. Susan's muff will be something else—dark blonde, Cleo guesses, the curls as fine as silk. Susan is lovely, coquettish in a way that makes Cleo suspects the girl wants to be dominated. Maybe she's not a true bottom, but just close enough to excite Cleo's imagination. Cleo wonders who the girl knows, who she's been with. She imagines Susan begging for things, begging for pleasure. What a pretty slave she'd make, Cleo thinks. The idea arouses Cleo because she enjoys exerting power over her women. She finds enough women who want it, and it's always thrilling with girls like Susan. Get them begging for it.

Cleo rises now and walks over to the buffet

against the wall, and opens a drawer. She brings out a camera and a pack of film. "I'd like to take some pictures of you," she says. "Let's find out how good a model you are."

Susan doesn't mind. Cleo keeps up a constant chatter about how pretty Susan is, and Susan obviously enjoys that, smiling at Cleo, tilting her head like a coquette. Yes, she likes the idea of posing.

Cleo shoots a few pictures of Susan reclined on the sofa, Susan looking demure. Getting sweaty, Cleo takes off her shirt and she now wears only a T-shirt and jeans, the exposure of her bare arms revealing a tattoo on her right biceps, a heart pierced by an arrow. Susan stares at the tattoo but she says nothing. Cleo picks up the camera again, points it at Susan and looks through the viewfinder. "Sexy girl," Cleo says. "Show us some more leg."

Susan giggles, teasing, tugging her dress back enough to show more of her thighs to the camera. She pulls her shoulders back to emphasize the curves of her breasts under the cotton dress. Cleo tells her to open her legs more and Susan does that, raising her knees, allowing the hem of her dress to fall back far enough to show the tops of her thighs. Now, when she opens her legs, the crotch of her blue panties is suddenly revealed.

"Yes, that's good," Cleo says, one eye fixed on the viewfinder as she snaps another picture, Susan's open thighs in the viewfinder, the blue panty-crotch bulging with the girl's pussy. Susan moves her legs. Her face is flushed, and Cleo guesses that the girl is getting turned on by the picture taking. Cleo knows. She has done this often enough with her women to know how some of them start creaming in response to the camera. Now she's wondering what Susan tastes like, aching to have the girl's nectar on her tongue.

"Take the dress off, honey. Let's get a few shots with more zip in them."

Susan giggles. "Am I going to be embarrassed by these pictures someday?"

"I'll give you the negatives."

"Promise?"

"Sure, doll. You trust me, don't you?" Cleo's excitement increases as she watches Susan rise and unzip the back of her dress. The girl does a slow striptease, gradually revealing her lithe body covered now by only a blue bra and blue panties, the cups of the bra with filmy lacework, the panties cut high on the sides and back to show much of her compact buttocks. She does a turn for Cleo, poses standing for several shots. Then, at Cleo's urging, Susan removes the bra to expose her darling breasts whose extended pink nipples testify that her excitement is as great as Cleo's.

The older woman now puts the camera down and approaches the girl, who waits for her with laughing eyes. "You're going to jump me," Susan says, pretending to cover her breasts with her hands but making sure to leave her nipples exposed between her spread fingers.

But it's not the girl's breasts Cleo wants. When Cleo is close enough, she slides her left arm around Susan's shoulders and kisses her mouth at the same time as her right hand moves directly to the blue panties. Susan gasps against Cleo's lips as Cleo's long fingers slip inside the crotch of her panties and pull the crotch outward as her knuckles rub into the wet groove of the girl's cunt.

Without haste, Cleo finds the shaft of Susan's clitoris and pinches it gently. "How about dressing up for me?"

Her eyes closed as she feels her clitoris being manipulated, Susan groans. "What do you mean?"

"I've got some stockings and heels you can wear. We'll take a few hot pictures."

"Only if you promise I get the negatives."

"I've already promised," Cleo says, pulling her hand away now and lifting it to her mouth where she slowly cleans Susan's nectar off her fingers. Susan blushes as she watches the older woman lick her froth. Cleo smiles and leaves her, walking out of the living room and down the short hall to the bedroom to find something Susan can wear. She returns to Susan with a white lace garter belt and sheer white hose and white high-heeled sandals, smiling at Susan when she sees Susan has already removed her blue panties to reveal her lovely triangle of silky blonde hair.

Susan blushes as she stares at the shoes and stockings in Cleo's hands. "You're different," Susan says.

"How so?"

"I've never done anything like this. I mean, wearing that stuff for someone."

Cleo chuckles, her eyes on the blonde pussy. "But you're going to like it, aren't you?"

"Yes, I think so."

"Come on, I'll help you." She helps Susan hook the garter belt around her loins. Then she assists Susan in getting the stockings on her legs. As Susan raises one leg after the other, Cleo's attention is drawn to the girl's blonde pussy, the visible pink stripe between the plump outer lips. Susan's tender breasts look like pomegranates as she bends forward to attach the garters to the tops of the sheer white stockings.

Susan says, "I'm feeling sexy with this stuff."

"You look sexy, too. Now the shoes, doll." It's the shoes—the high-heeled sandals—that bring a special pleasure to Cleo. She slips them onto Susan's feet, and then she buckles the straps across the girl's pretty ankles.

When Susan finally rises, she giggles as she balances herself on the four-inch stiletto heels. "Let me look in the mirror."

Cleo watches Susan as she walks across the living room to the full-length mirror in the short hall near the front door. The high heels, the long slender body, make Susan look ravishing. Cleo takes up the camera and she begins snapping pictures again, Susan at the mirror with her lips pouting as she looks at herself, Susan turning to glance at the curves of her buttocks framed by the white garter belt, Susan assuming a model's pose with one leg gracefully bent at the knee. Cleo's desire increases, and before long she stops taking pictures of Susan and stands there, rubbing her cunt through her jeans as she watches Susan twist and turn her body in various poses.

Cleo finally takes the girl's arm. "Come back to the living room."

Susan giggles as she allows herself to be led along. Because of the high heels, she's now taller than Cleo, tall enough so that when Cleo wants to kiss her, Susan needs to bend her head to meet Cleo's lips.

Cleo drops a hand down to stroke Susan's ass. "Let me take some pictures of your pussy."

Susan giggles. "I thought it was coming to that." But Susan doesn't mind. She enjoys it. She stands near one of the easy chairs and lifts one foot to place it on the seat cushion, her legs now wide apart to show everything to Cleo, who quickly grabs the camera to take a picture of Susan's lovely cunt pouting open like a pink flower, the dew glistening on the petals, her clitoris still modestly covered by its hood. As if understanding completely what Cleo wants, Susan slides a hand between her legs and uses her fingers to tug the cowl back and expose the tip of her clitoris.

"That's perfect," Cleo says. When Susan starts playing with herself, rubbing her cunt with her fingers, Cleo takes another picture. Their eyes meet. Susan blushes, but she continues to masturbate as Cleo watches her. The girl wobbles on the high heels, her tongue sliding over her lips, her breasts jerking with each movement of the hand between her legs. Cleo laughs, and she finally stops it. She makes Susan turn around under the pretext of adjusting the straps of the garter belt. Cleo fondles Susan's ass, and then she gets her fingers between Susan's buttocks to stroke her anus. Susan giggles, enjoying it, showing her small white teeth as she laughs. "You're making me nutty," Susan says, wagging her hips from side to side as Cleo's fingers probe inside her wet cunt.

Cleo picks up the camera again. "Let's have a picture of that lovely butt." She makes Susan bend forward to emphasize her ass. With a little more coaxing, Susan reaches back to pull her buttocks apart to show her cunt and anus from behind. "You're being nasty," Susan says.

"Yes, but I can tell you like it."

"Why don't you get undressed and let me suck you off?" Cleo quivers and she slaps Susan's buttocks. "Now who's being nasty? Do you like sucking off old dykes?"

"Only if they taste good."

Cleo slaps her ass again. "You're a little bitch, aren't you? All right, lie down on the rug."

Susan quickly stretches out on the rug as Cleo removes her jeans and underpants. Cleo's cunt is wet, her pulse racing as she gazes down at the girl waiting for her. Holding her crotch with her hand, Cleo straddles Susan's body, and then she squats down to fit her cunt against Susan's upturned mouth.

"Good girl," Cleo says, and she starts grinding her

crotch against Susan's face, rubbing her clit against Susan's nose and lips and chin as she wonders how far she can go with Susan and whether Susan will ever come back to her. Sometimes they never come back. You pine for them, but they never come back. They walk into your life one day, and then they walk out again, and for them you're only an anecdote.

"Come on, suck it," Cleo says, her eyes making contact with Susan's eyes as she adds a twist to the movement of her cunt.

# FIVE

# Valerie

The next day Valerie arrives at Cleo's apartment wearing a dress and heels. Hot kisses follow once the front door is closed. And then Cleo discovers the gartered stockings and she goes wild. "Come on, show me."

In the living room, Valerie holds her dress up to show her legs and thighs, the tops of her stockings, the black lace garter belt. The lace panties are already soaked. Cleo makes her walk around like that. And then finally Cleo rushes her into the bedroom and tumbles her onto the bed. The older woman hurries to get Valerie's panties off. She slips her thighs under Valerie's ass and pushes her knees back to her breasts to make Valerie's crotch spread out like a banquet, everything available. Valerie has never before had it like this. Cleo's full control drives her wild. Cleo's tongue probes between her labia, slithering, sucking at the mouth of her vagina.

Valerie moans, shudders at the hot stabbing of Cleo's tongue.

"Do you like this, doll?"

"Yes."

"Up a little more. Yes, that's better. Keep those pretty legs up."

Valerie's high heels wave in the air. Cleo bends her head again, her tongue wagging, her thumbs spreading Valerie's flower to get at her clit. Miss Pearl coming out of her hood. Valerie shudders as she watches the woman slurp the juice oozing out of her pussy. The noises. Cleo slobbering like that. Cleo pushing her knees back as she presses her chin against Valerie's ass.

And Valerie thinks: It's Frankie who ought to be doing this. She's Frankie's woman, not Cleo's. But at this moment she's totally Cleo's woman. Spread for Cleo, isn't she? But still Frankie ought to be doing it. She's Frankie's wife. Frankie ought to know how much she needs this. Loving like this. At least once in a while. The bitch Frankie takes better care of her books than she does of her wife. Frankie never sucks her like this. Making a meal out of her. Driving her crazy.

Now Cleo has Valerie's cunt in her mouth. Literally. Chewing on a lip, pulling it inside her mouth, sucking the swollen flap. Valerie thinks her clit feels bigger than ever before, puffed, turgid, throbbing. When Cleo finally starts sucking her clit, Valerie throws her head back and groans. Oh, God, yes. Suck it. Suck my clit. Cleo grips Valerie's ass with both hands, pushing her thumbs inside Valerie's cunt to stretch it wide open. Then more sucking on Valerie's clit until her cunt explodes. Cleo holds on, not releasing her, keeping Valerie's cunt captured.

When Valerie opens her eyes again, she finds Cleo smiling at her.

Cleo says, "You enjoyed that, didn't you?"

"Yes." Cleo is sitting in a lotus position, her legs folded, her knees wide open, her slit gaping at Valerie, the older woman's cunt hypnotizing her.

"I think you've been doing without," Cleo says. "You shouldn't. It's bad for you. Makes you crazy." Her hand strokes Valerie's nylon-clad ankle. Then the shoe. Running her fingertips over the spike heel. "Anyway, I like you. I want you to know that."

Valerie blushes. "I like you, too." Then Cleo wants to know how committed she is to Frankie. And Valerie has to explain how she isn't thinking of leaving Frankie just yet because she's hoping things will work out. Develop. Change. A transformation of some kind. Why not? People change, don't they? With her eyes on Cleo's pink pussy. So unavoidable because there it is staring at her as Cleo sits with her knees wide open.

Cleo smiles when she notices Valerie's eyes on her cunt. "You want to do me?" And, without waiting for an answer, she climbs over Valerie, squats over Valerie's face, then drops her pussy down until Valerie has the pink slash of Cleo's cunt on her mouth, Cleo immediately groaning, sliding back and forth, holding onto the headboard with her hands as she mashes her wet cunt against Valerie's face while telling Valerie how much she likes her.

Later Cleo fucks Valerie with her fingers. Valerie is hoping they can do a little cunt-rubbing because she likes that with lanky women, but Cleo wants to use her fingers instead. So Valerie lies back with her knees up while Cleo uses those long fingers to make her come three times. Hard fucking that leaves Valerie's cunt bruised by Cleo's knuckles. Cleo offers to get her fist inside, but Valerie says no, she's had enough. Next time, Cleo says. Next time she'll show Valerie how good it is with all of her hand inside

Valerie's cunt. "You'll go wild," Cleo says. "I'm very good with my hand."

"You look anxious," Jay says. Jay is Valerie's closest friend. Valerie worked as a schoolteacher for two years after finishing college, and she met Jay at the school. Neither one of them had come out yet, and connecting was difficult, awkward, and a great secret. But they actually made love only once, one of those affairs that never go anywhere. But after that they became constant friends, kept in touch, and Valerie has always enjoyed Jay's company. Now, in a downtown coffee shop, Valerie feels a need to unburden herself as she tells Jay everything, all about her troubles with Frankie and the new woman Cleo.

When Valerie finishes talking, Jay raises an eyebrow and says, "I think I know this Cleo."

"You do?"

"You know I don't do the bar scene, but I think I met her at some groups. Is she in the trucking business?"

"Yes."

"Then it must be her. I've heard she's nasty."

"What do you mean?"

"She's into pushing her lovers around. What are you going to do now?"

Blushing, Valerie says she has no idea. She isn't thinking of leaving Frankie because she loves Frankie. Jay knows Frankie and likes her. Jay is living with a lover now, another schoolteacher. Valerie says she won't leave Frankie, but she certainly isn't happy with her life. "I'm having a rough time."

Jay tilts her head to the side and says things will work themselves out. "There's nothing wrong with some playtime on the side," Jay says. "Provided you keep it from Frankie."

"I don't like doing it."

"No one likes doing it. Unless they need it."

That's it, isn't it? If she needs it and she can't get it at home, she has to do it in order to have a life.

"Anyway, be careful with Cleo," Jay says. "Don't let her push you around too much."

Which makes Valerie blush again, because it's the pushing around that makes her like Cleo so much.

"My sweet doll," Cleo says. She has Valerie on her bed, both of them naked, Valerie on her back with her knees up as Cleo now mounts her. Holding her knees with her hands, Valerie watches the older woman position herself to get their cunts kissing. A moment later, Valerie moans as Cleo begins a twisting grind that sends flashes of hot pleasure through Valerie's pussy and belly. Cleo humps and churns, grinding their pubic bones one against the other, then pulling back to hoist Valerie's legs over her shoulders. Now, supporting the upper part of her body with her hands, Cleo starts fucking her again.

"How does it feel, doll?"

Valerie moans. Her pubis feels bruised, her cunt on fire. "I love it."

Cleo laughs, moves again, thrusting forcefully against Valerie's pussy. She pushes Valerie's legs away and lies flat on Valerie's body. With her weight on Valerie, she starts grinding again, the two juicy cunts slamming against each other. Valerie's belly is soaked, drenched with their juices.

Then Cleo slips her fingers inside Valerie's cunt, fucking her now with two fingers in her vagina, her hips bouncing up and down as her fingers slide in and out of Valerie's canal. The penetration is deep, total, a vigorous possession that Valerie adores. She loves being taken like this by a woman, the force of it, the overwhelming force of the body above her own. She loves having a woman fuck her like this, the woman's fingers stretching her cunt wide open. She begs Cleo for more of it, more hard fucking. She cries out as Cleo's long fingers ravage her vagina. She has no doubt this is right, this fucking outside her relationship with Frankie. Her lover Frankie. All she cares about at this moment is the pleasure she feels, the skill Cleo has in satisfying her. Cleo pounds her now, slamming Valerie's knees back against her breasts, pumping her fingers inside Valerie's vagina.

Suddenly Cleo pulls her fingers out, smiling. "Roll over, doll."

Valerie groans, dismayed by the abrupt absence of Cleo's fingers. Blushing, obedient, she rolls over onto her belly. She quivers with excitement. Cleo pulls at her waist to get her up on her knees. Valerie's head rests on the pillow, her ass in the air, her body totally vulnerable. Kneeling behind her, Cleo fingers Valerie's cunt, pulls the lips apart and tells her how lovely she looks. "Red and dripping," Cleo says. "Tasty white frosting all over it."

Valerie shudders. What a thrill it is to be taken like this. She adores the total animality. This is the ultimate, the most basic kind of woman-fucking, her cunt and ass presented to Cleo, her two openings available, offered. This is what she needs, what Frankie never gives her.

She trembles, waiting, not knowing what Cleo will do next. Maybe Cleo will take her ass. Something never done by Frankie. Valerie tells herself she wouldn't mind it. She likes it when it's done right. The pleasure can be intense. She weaves her hips from side to side, silently urging Cleo to do something.

One hand rubbing the small of Valerie's back,

Cleo slowly pushes two fingers inside Valerie's cunt again. She leans over Valerie's body as she penetrates deep inside her vagina. Valerie whimpers as Cleo slides her hand underneath to grasp one of her hanging breasts. Cleo pinches the stiff nipple as her long fingers piston in and out of Valerie's cunt. Valerie cries out, grinding her ass against Cleo's belly, her juices gushing as Cleo fucks her. Waves of pleasure rush up her chest as her cunt spasms, a hot flood over her body, an intense orgasm.

Cleo continues thrusting in her cunt, and then finally she pulls her fingers out and wipes them on Valerie's ass. "Come on top of me, honey. Let's try it that way."

Valerie groans, wound up like a tight wire, willing to do anything Cleo wants, anything to keep them fucking.

Cleo lies down on her back, and Valerie squats over her belly. Cleo spreads Valerie's cunt with her fingers, and then she slips the fingers inside to take her again.

Valerie rides the older woman's fingers, gyrating her hips, moaning as the fingers stabs her canal. She can feel her juices gushing out. She whimpers with pleasure as Cleo's free hand squeezes one of her breasts.

Cleo chuckles. "Come on, doll, move it. Fuck my fingers."

Valerie groans. "That's what I'm doing."

"Would you like to piss a little? Do it on my hand. I get turned on when a girl pisses on my hand while I'm fucking her."

"Cleo, please...."

"Don't you want to?"

Valerie giggles. "That's too much."

"Come on, just a little bit."

"No, I can't!" She won't do it, not with Cleo. It's too raunchy, too vulgar. She continues grinding her ass, squatting over Cleo as she fucks Cleo's stiff fingers, but she refuses to do what Cleo wants.

Grasping one of Valerie's breasts, Cleo pulls her forward and hunches upward. She pumps her fingers in and out of Valerie's cunt. Valerie moans as Cleo pummels her clit. Now Cleo releases Valerie's breast to grab her ass. Her fingers slice between Valerie's buttocks to probe her anus. Valerie cries out as she feels herself penetrated in both places, Cleo's fingers in her cunt and ass, a total possession as she continues to squat over Cleo with her juices running out to drench both of them. She comes hard, gasping, whimpering, then finally rolling over on her side exhausted.

Cleo takes Valerie in her arms and kisses her, soothing kisses on her eyes and forehead. "You came so hard for me, I love you." Her hands knead Valerie's buttocks, her strong fingers pressing into Valerie's flesh. Valerie cuddles against her, flushed and happy, her lips pressed against Cleo's neck as Cleo continues fondling her ass.

"Do you want the blanket?"

"No, I'm fine," Valerie says.

"Are you sure?"

"Yes."

One of Cleo's fingers finds Valerie's anus and slips inside. "You're so tight."

"Oh, Cleo...."

"I can tell you like it."

Valerie whimpers against Cleo's neck. "I don't like it when it hurts."

"Am I hurting you now?"

"No."

"Does it belong to me?"

"Cleo, please...."

"Say it."

"Yes."

Cleo chuckles and kisses her mouth. Valerie wants it. She wants everything Cleo wants. Maybe it's revenge against Frankie. If Cleo wants her ass, Valerie will give it to her. Her anus is already twitching around Cleo's invading finger, but the opening is still too dry. "Cleo, use something."

Cleo agrees, says she has some lotion she can use. She brings the bottle from the night table, and Valerie trembles as she lies on her side and watches Cleo spread the lotion over her long fingers. Valerie can feel the heat in her face. She's uncertain again as she imagines those long fingers inside her.

Then Cleo makes her lift one leg, draw the knee up to her chest. Cleo squeezes out another glob of lotion, and this time she paints Valerie's anus with it. Valerie groans, her eyes closed as Cleo's finger slowly pushes inside her lubricated ass.

"You're still tight," Cleo says. "Come on, relax for me, honey." Her finger stretches the tight ring, slowly sliding in and out.

The intimacy of the act makes Valerie shudder with pleasure. Yes, she does want this. She wants to be taken this way. The lubrication makes it easy, and the pleasure is already intense. Cleo is gentle as she stretches her opening, whispering to her, asking her if it's good, does she like it? Telling her she can feel she's relaxing now. Cleo adds a second finger, pushes the second finger inside Valerie's ass, pushes both fingers deep inside the passage as she urges Valerie to open up to her. Valerie moans as she does her best to remain open and loose to the invading digits, gasping at intervals as the two fingers slide in and out of her ass. Cleo is gentle and forceful at the same time. Valerie's ass is now receptive, yielding, craving those long fingers to do more. She's thrilled by it now, shuddering as Cleo kisses her again, as Cleo holds her tightly with her free arm, whispering in her ear, calling her a hot-ass bitch. Valerie loves it. She loves all of it. She loves everything about Cleo.

"Come for me, honey. Come for Cleo now."

Valerie cries out, jerks her hips back and forth, and comes hard as her ass clutches at Cleo's fingers.

# Frankie

At two o'clock in the afternoon, Frankie is sitting in the waiting room of Dr. Virginia Fay. Three other people are in the room, three expensively dressed middle-aged women, each with a magazine on her lap, each woman idly turning the pages of the magazine with a light rustling sound. The shadow of the receptionist can be seen behind the glass partition.

Frankie is annoyed. This is only her second visit—a new gynecologist for her—and when she made the appointment, the girl on the phone assured her she would not need to wait, assured her that Dr. Fay understood the needs of professionals and how important it was not to waste time during the working day. Understands nothing, Frankie thinks. Dr. Fay was recommended to Frankie by Sandy Edberg, a female attorney acquaintance of Frankie's. Not a friend, merely an acquaintance, but maybe Sandy understands Frankie is gay. The first visit to Dr. Fay six months ago was uneventful and routine, and at least there hadn't been any waiting that time. Frankie hates waiting in waiting rooms. Restless, she squirms on her chair, picks up a magazine, puts it down again, fidgets with her watchband.

Finally the glass window slides open, and the face of the receptionist appears. "Ms. Hooper?"

In a few minutes, Frankie is alone in a small examining room, seated on the cushioned examining table, waiting again, her clothes on a clothes tree and her body covered by a green cotton gown. The door opens and Dr. Fay walks in, a tall, efficient-looking woman of forty in a white coat.

Dr. Fay smiles. "And how are we today?"

"I'm fine," Frankie says. The doctor makes small talk as she takes Frankie's blood pressure, chitchat about the weather, the traffic on the Outer Drive, the latest exhibit at the Art Institute.

"How's the love life?" Dr. Fay says. "Are we taking proper precautions these days?"

"Yes."

"Are you seeing one man exclusively?"

Frankie hesitates. "I'm gay, doctor."

Flustered, Dr. Fay pulls the stethoscope out of her ears and slips it into one of the pockets of her coat. She avoids Frankie's eyes. "Sorry about that. I didn't notice it on your card. I'll be back in a few minutes for the pelvic."

And she leaves. Frankie is now alone again, irritated by the room, the doctor, her gown, the mushy feel of the examining table underneath her buttocks. She hates doctors and hospitals and all things medical. She has memories of herself as a child screaming during examinations by physicians. She tells herself that Dr. Fay ought to have known she's gay because

she made a point of telling her during the first visit.
Stupid bitch in a white coat, Frankie thinks. She wonders how much trouble she'll have finding another
gynecologist.

The door opens and the nurse enters, a thin young
woman with dark eyes, unappealing, already pegged
by Frankie during the first visit as a dyke. The nurse
wants Frankie to lie down and get ready for the pelvic
exam. The nurse brings up the stirrups from the sides
of the table; and then, when Frankie lies down on her
back, she lifts Frankie's ankles into place. "That's
good," the nurse says, and Frankie gets a small rush
as the nurse gives Frankie's cunt an extended look of
interest, Frankie imagines the nurse's face buried in it
with her long dyke tongue flapping around to make
her feel good. But the nurse is too unappealing, and
Frankie avoids eye contact, amusing herself by imagining what it would be like to be a nurse and look at
cunts all day. Marcia only shrugged when Frankie
asked, but of course Marcia is a psychiatric nurse and
doesn't get much chance to look at cunts.

Now the door opens and the doctor comes in to
examine Frankie. Brusque, efficient, hardly a glance
at Frankie's face. Is she more distant than the last
time? Does she remember that a short while ago
Frankie told her she's gay? Frankie thinks that
maybe Dr. Fay is more distant because of that, Dr.
Fay with a dyke nurse but not gay herself, or if she is
gay she doesn't advertise, her fingers now doing
things to Frankie's cunt, taking a smear, probing,
pulling, almost getting her nose in it as she bends forward with that light on her forehead that makes her
look like a fugitive from a science-fiction movie. Is
she gay? Oh, fuck, I don't care, Frankie thinks. All
she wants now is to get out of here. She doesn't like
the routine here. The other gynecologist had a

smoother setup. Maybe she just hates the idea of strange women looking at her cunt.

"You're fine," Dr. Fay says, sliding back on her chair, then rising. "Assuming the Pap smear is negative, I'll see you in six months." A short smile at Frankie, and then she leaves.

Well, the Pap had better be negative, hadn't it? The nurse gets Frankie's ankles off the stirrups, gets her legs down, but instead of leaving, she dawdles. "Was it raining when you came in?"

"No, not at all."

"I never remember to bring my umbrella."

Frankie wants the nurse to leave before she removes the gown and gets dressed. She sits on the table and waits, but the nurse insists on puttering in one of the cabinets.

The nurse says, "On some days this job is a pain."

Frankie doesn't answer, pretends she has nothing to say, waits for the nurse to leave, and finally the nurse mutters something else and she walks out.

Dumb bitch, Frankie thinks.

Later that afternoon, Frankie is in her office when her secretary buzzes her. "There's a Miss Marcia Mason here. Says she's one of your clients."

Frankie curses under her breath. "All right, show her in and hold my calls."

In a moment, Marcia enters the office and closes the door behind her. "You don't mind, do you? I got off work early, and I thought I could drop by."

Frankie does her best to sound pleasant. "It's better if you telephone first."

Instead of sitting down, Marcia walks over to where Frankie is seated behind her desk, and she bends forward to kiss Frankie's lips. "Don't be angry with me, I just wanted to see you."

76

"I'm not angry," Frankie says, apprehensive now because she's afraid to get caught with Marcia by the others in her office. Frankie rises. She goes to the door to lock it. Now she feels more secure, and when she returns to Marcia, she leads Marcia away from the window and kisses her. "I don't usually bring my personal life into the office, pet."

"I'm sorry."

"Never mind, you're here already." The fact is, Frankie isn't that displeased now that she has Marcia standing so close to her she can smell Marcia's perfume and look down at the ripe swells of Marcia's breasts in her scoop-neck peasant blouse. "You're not wearing a bra," Frankie says.

Marcia giggles. "That's right." They kiss again, and this time Frankie gets her hands on Marcia's lovely full breasts, enjoying the feel of them after the rotten day she's had. She gets one of Marcia's breasts over the top of the blouse and starts sucking it, Marcia encouraging her by holding the tit with her hand and making noises of pleasure as Frankie's lips tug at the fat nipple. "God, I love the way you do that!" Marcia says.

Her mouth fixed on the tip of the large breast, Frankie slides a hand under Marcia's billowing skirt to find the sopping crotch of Marcia's pantyhose. Her fingers insistent, probing, forceful, Frankie rubs Marcia's plump cunt until Marcia groans and comes.

"Oh, Jesus!" Marcia gasps.

"Come on, let's get out of here. I'll tell them I'm leaving early."

In Marcia's apartment, Marcia lies naked on her bed with her breasts lolling on her chest like a pair of balloons and a Panasonic Special buzzing between her spread legs. The vibrator has a huge disc-shaped head rimmed with black rubber, angled by Marcia now so the edge of the disc pushes between her labia. Marcia moans, her face sweaty, her knees shaking at intervals as the pleasure tears through her cunt.

Frankie sits on a chair near the bed. She's wearing an undershirt and underpants, what she had on under her suit when she arrived with Marcia. Nothing much has happened yet, except that Marcia is ignoring Frankie and having fun with her vibrator, which makes Frankie think that maybe Marcia is too much for her, too sexually uncontrolled. She doesn't mind Marcia's using the vibrator, what she minds is just watching it without doing anything. She's also a little amazed at the way Marcia appears to be having a continuous orgasm. When Frankie uses a vibrator, she comes in spurts—bang, bang, bang, not one continuous convulsion. She hasn't ever done it with Valerie, not with a vibrator. They've used dildos, but nothing electrical. The fact is, vibrators make Frankie unhappy because she thinks they're much too mechanical. She would rather use her mouth and fingers on a woman than something you plug into a wall.

Frankie finally leaves the chair. She crouches to pull the vibrator plug out of the electric outlet in the wall.

Marcia suddenly cries out, looks at the dead vibrator and then looks at Frankie. "Hey, what the hell is going on?"

"Either you put that thing away or I leave," Frankie says.

Marcia giggles. "You're kidding."

"No, I'm not kidding."

Frankie climbs on the bed. She takes the vibrator

out of Marcia's hands and puts it on the night table. Then she spreads Marcia's legs and gets her b.ody between Marcia's thighs with her pubic bone mashed against Marcia's cunt.

"Oh, yeah," Marcia says. She lifts her knees, but Frankie wants them down. When Frankie has the arrangement she wants, she begins grinding her cunt against Marcia's cunt, a steady slow fucking with Frankie's underpants quickly drenched by Marcia's flowing juices.

Marcia comes, but it's not enough for her. When Frankie pulls back, Marcia rolls over onto her knees. "Do it to me like this."

Frankie's excitement increases as she gazes at Marcia's hairy cunt and ass. Marcia has more hair down there than most women. Frankie strokes Marcia's buttocks. She tickles the plump cunt. Then she spreads the lips apart with her fingers and gets her tongue on Marcia's clit. The chunky brunette presses backward, attempting to get more pressure on her clit, moaning now as Frankie begins a steady lapping of the running cunt, her tongue lapping up and down as she licks up the rich flowing juices.

"Come on, rim me," Marcia says. But Frankie has no interest in it, and she's also a bit resentful that Marcia asks for it. Frankie can't remember anyone who actually asked her for it. Rimming is something you do or don't do, but it should be up to the rimmer, Frankie thinks. Instead, she sucks Marcia's cunt with more vigor, getting her tongue inside the vaginal opening and fluttering it in and out as Marcia squeals and humps her ass back at Frankie's face.

Later, as she gets dressed, Frankie thinks maybe she ought to end it with Marcia. Maybe it's time to end it because Marcia is really too much for her. But she says nothing to Marcia. At the door she kisses Marcia good-by and squeezes one of Marcia's breasts.

That evening, as Frankie and Valerie sit together in the living room, Valerie says, "Can I ask you something?"

"What is it?"

"Is there something going on between us?"

"If there is, I don't know about it."

"I have the feeling something's going on."

"There's nothing going on."

"It's like you never have time for me."

"You're talking about sex."

"Yes."

"Valerie, you know how busy I am."

"That's what I mean—you're always busy."

"You're being silly again. I'm no busier now than I was when we first met. I'm in a busy profession."

Valerie says nothing. She returns to flipping the pages of her magazine, one of her crossed legs swinging like a metronome.

Two hours later, Frankie is standing in the hallway outside their bedroom. The bedroom door is open just a crack, but it's enough so she can see into the room, see everything clearly, see Valerie on the bed in her pink nightgown that Frankie thinks is too cute, Valerie with her knees up, the nightgown pulled back, her right hand between her thighs and her fingers in her cunt.

Frankie watches it. She could walk in and interrupt her, or she can stand here and watch it. She chooses to watch it, wondering whether maybe Valerie expects it, wondering why she feels differently about Valerie these days. In the beginning Frankie told herself this was it: Valerie was everything she wanted, they would be happy forever and ever, and nothing would ever come between them. Now she watches the jerking movement of Valerie's hand, and she wonders why she was ever so naïve about Valerie, so naïve about what she herself wants out of life.

# SEVEN

# **Valerie**

"It makes me feel uncomfortable," Valerie says to Cleo. They sit opposite each other in a booth in a restaurant.

It's two o'clock in the afternoon, and Valerie is uncomfortable because for the past ten minutes Cleo has been asking her questions about her sex life with Frankie. Valerie thinks it's disloyal to talk about Frankie to Cleo, but one part of her mind tells her she's being silly because the worse disloyalty is the way she secretly has sex with Cleo behind Frankie's back.

Cleo says, "You mean it makes you hot."

Valerie blushes. "I didn't say that. I said it makes me uncomfortable to talk about Frankie behind her back."

"I thought you liked me."

"I do, Cleo. I like you a lot."

"But not enough to tell me what you do with Frankie."

Valerie groans. She looks around the restaurant one more time to make sure none of Frankie's friends are in the room. She wasn't happy when Cleo suggested this place, but now that they're here, there isn't much she can do about it. "We don't do anything unusual. Anyway, I don't know why it's so important to talk about it."

Cleo smirks, glancing at Valerie, and then at the waitress as she walks by their table. "It's important because it interests me. Has she ever fisted you?"

Valerie feels the flush in her face. "No."

"When was the last time you did anything together."

"Saturday night." Cleo chuckles. "Oh, yeah. Wednesdays and Saturdays, isn't it? What did you do with her?"

"Cleo, please...."

"You know you're going to tell me. Just tell me what you did with her."

And so Valerie describes to Cleo what happened between her and Frankie on Saturday night, how they went out to dinner and then afterward made love for a change in the living room, Frankie insisting that Valerie kneel on the sofa while Frankie fucked her from behind with her fingers.

Cleo looks amused. "Did you like it?"

"Yes, of course I did."

"And what did you do after that? Did you go down on her?"

Valerie blushes. "No, we just went to sleep."

"That's all? What's her cunt like? Does she have a big clit?"

"Cleo, please...."

"Please what, honey?"

"Please keep your voice down—we're in a restaurant."

"Hell, I know that. All I'm thinking about now is getting my tongue a mile up your cunt and wiggling it around. Would you like that?"

"Oh, God."

In Cleo's cluttered tiny bathroom, Valerie has her panties off and her skirt hiked up to her waist as she bends forward over the toilet to show Cleo her ass.

"My precious doll," Cleo says. Valerie groans as she supports her weight with one hand on the tank behind the toilet. "You always get me so hot."

She feels Cleo's hand on her ass, Cleo's fingers sliding between her buttocks to find her cunt. Valerie moans as Cleo spreads the petals and teases her with a tickling fingertip.

"Don't move," Cleo says. Valerie's heart beats wildly as she imagines what she looks like bent over like this with her ass naked. A gasp comes out of her throat as she feels Cleo tickling her anus.

"Cleo, please...."

"I said, 'Don't move.'" They've done this on other occasions, and by now Valerie is used to it. Cleo's games. Valerie hears Cleo open the medicine cabinet, and a moment later she feels something cool on her anus, a lubricant jelly, always effective enough so that when Cleo pushes a finger inside her, Valerie can take it without difficulty.

"My thumb," Cleo says with a soft laugh, the digit now wriggling in Valerie's rectum as Cleo's forefinger and middle finger slide effortlessly inside Valerie's wet vagina. "There, I've got you," Cleo says, her three fingers hooked inside Valerie two openings as if to hold a bowling ball. "Go on, move it, honey. Show Cleo how that ass can move."

Valerie loves it. She groans, the intense excitement producing a raging fire in her belly, a fire only augmented by the desperate embarrassment she feels, the awareness of her complete surrender to Cleo's will.

She moves her ass. Cleo taunted her during the ride home by telling her how they would do it, how Valerie would move her ass against Cleo's fingers; and now here they are making it real, Valerie humping her ass against Cleo's firm hand in order to fuck herself on Cleo's invading fingers. Valerie groans and grunts, desperately seeking an orgasm, arching her back as she thrusts her ass and cunt at Cleo's fingers. Cleo laughs as Valerie finally comes, as Valerie cries out and shakes her hips from side to side.

Her fingers remaining embedded in Valerie's two canals, Cleo says, "Good, baby? Come on, clamp down a little more and finish it."

Valerie is always amazed at the way Cleo understands everything about her body and the way it works, what brings the most pleasure when they fuck. She clamps her two holes on Cleo's fingers, groaning as she feels another squirt of bliss in her cunt. Cleo then slowly withdraws her fingers, and she makes Valerie drop her dress and turn around. Cleo suggests that Valerie drop the skirt and just wear the stockings and heels. "You know how much I like looking at your legs," Cleo says.

Valerie is without a garter belt because the stockings have elastic tops. "What about my blouse?"

Cleo kisses her. "You can leave it on." And then she adds, "I've invited someone to join us, and she ought to be here soon."

Valerie is stunned. "Someone to join us?"

Cleo chuckles, her hand stroking Valerie's cheek. "Don't worry, doll, it just makes things better for us.

Her name is Susan, and she likes doing whatever she's told. Won't that be fun?"

Still dazed by the news that someone is about to join them, Valerie follows Cleo out of the bathroom and into the living room. There Cleo reminds Valerie about her skirt. With trembling fingers, Valerie unzips her skirt, drops it, steps out of it. The blouse she wears isn't long enough to cover her triangle, which puffs out in a dark thicket at the joining of her thighs. Cleo smiles with approval, and she makes Valerie do a turn to show her ass above the tops of the stockings. "You're delicious," Cleo says. "The shoes are new, aren't they?"

Valerie nods. Yes, the shoes are new, bought the day before on Oak Street because she had a date with Cleo and she knew Cleo would like them. Cleo does like them, and Valerie is happy that she's pleased her lover.

At that moment the front doorbell rings, and Cleo walks off to answer. When Cleo returns, she has Susan with her; Susan the tall college girl with dark blonde hair and a sultry beauty that Valerie immediately finds threatening.

"This is Susan," Cleo says, her eyes amused as she introduces them to each other.

Of course Susan's eyes are wide as she takes in Valerie's getup, the blouse and the stockings and heels and the exposed cunt. Susan wears long silver earrings and heels and a dress that Cleo wants removed at once. "Take it off," Cleo says, waving her hand at Susan in a way that makes Valerie understand that Susan is accustomed to taking such orders from Cleo.

Susan undresses without a word, unbuttoning her dress and then pulling it off her body with a single smooth movement. Under the dress, she wears only a white garter belt to hold up her stockings. Her pussy is shaved, the mound bald and shining, the upper part of her slit just visible between the plump outer lips.

"What do you think of her?" Cleo says to Valerie.

"She's beautiful," Valerie says.

Cleo laughs. "Oh, she's beautiful, all right. And she's also hot. Beautiful and hot." Cleo beckons to Susan and, when the girl comes forward, Cleo slides a hand between Susan's thighs to finger her bald cunt. When she pulls her fingers away, they glisten with Susan's juices, and with a laugh Cleo lifts her hand to Susan's mouth and makes Susan lick her fingers clean. "See that? Do you see how hot she is?"

In the bedroom, Cleo lies in the center of the bed with Susan and Valerie on each side of her and Cleo's arms around their shoulders. Susan lies on Cleo's right and Valerie on Cleo's left. Valerie has removed her blouse, but she still wears her stockings and heels. Susan wears what she wore in the living room; the white garter belt, beige stockings, and dainty Italian pumps. Cleo has removed most of her clothes, and she now wears only a white T-shirt.

The window shade is down, the room in gray shadows, the bodies on the bed almost indistinct. From the stereo in the living room, comes the voice of Carey Wilson singing a plaintive love song.

Cleo now pushes at Susan's head, and Susan obediently slides her body downward on the bed, downward until Cleo is able to lift her right leg and hook her knee over Susan's shoulder. After shifting her body again, Susan gets her face between Cleo's open thighs and she begins sucking Cleo's cunt.

Cleo murmurs something, or is it merely a chuckle of happiness? She grips Valerie's shoulder more firmly, pulling Valerie toward her and kissing Valerie's mouth. Valerie moans against Cleo's lips. Then Cleo releases Valerie, and again Valerie gazes down to watch Susan as she eats Cleo's cunt.

Susan's eyes are closed, her nose buried in Cleo's blonde bush, her face sliding from side to side as she uses her mouth to massage Cleo's sex.

Valerie feels an intense excitement as she watches it. Susan is obviously hungry, her eyes closed, her mouth sucking ravenously at Cleo's upward-tilted cunt. Does Cleo love Susan? Valerie realizes how jealous she is. She has such an enormous desire to please Cleo, and here she is watching another girl with her face between Cleo's legs. She wonders about Susan, wonders why Susan is so submissive. So far they've hardly said more than a few words to each other.

Cleo makes Susan stop what she is doing. She pushes Susan away with her foot and tells Valerie to get over her. She wants Valerie straddling her on all fours so she can get at Valerie's hanging breasts. Valerie does it, groaning as Cleo takes her dangling breasts in her hands, then shuddering with delight as Cleo orders Susan to get behind Valerie and do her ass. "Rim her," Cleo orders, and the next moment Valerie squeals with happiness as she feels Susan's face pressing against her ass and Susan's tongue licking at her anus.

The afternoon light has faded completely, and in Cleo's bedroom a small lamp is now lit. The three women are still on the bed, but Cleo is now lying on her right side while both Valerie and Susan lie with their heads toward Cleo's feet. Susan lies behind Cleo with her face pushing between Cleo's buttocks. Valerie is on the other side, her mouth occupied with Cleo's cunt while Susan pays homage to Cleo's ass.

Muttering softly, Cleo slowly moves her loins backward and forward against the two mouths.

Valerie adores it. She loves the heady nectar flowing out of Cleo's cunt. At intervals her forehead touches Susan's forehead, making Valerie more aware of Susan's presence, Susan's tongue so close at the other opening, the sucking sounds made by Susan's lips.

But Valerie is also afraid. She's afraid Cleo will make her as submissive as Susan, make her a body slave like sweet Susan. Is it possible? Valerie shudders as she listens to the sucking sounds made by Susan's lips.

# EIGHT

# **Frankie**

At three o'clock in the afternoon in a large downtown auditorium, the Illinois Bar Association gathers to honor one of its own. Frankie arrives early and she decides to take a seat up front. She hopes maybe sitting near the dais will force her to keep her eyes open. These gatherings of attorneys are a professional necessity, but always so insufferably boring. Is there anything more boring than a pontificating attorney?

Gradually the seats in the auditorium begin to be occupied, blue and gray suits worn by both the men and the women, an occasional flamboyant sport jacket adorning a flamboyant trial lawyer. As the noise in the room increases, Frankie opens the New York Times to read about the latest Wall Street scandal. She hopes the paper will screen her from old law-school acquaintances she has no desire to meet again.

When the meeting begins, Frankie puts the newspaper away and listens to a succession of speakers reviewing significant local events in the legal profession. Frankie takes notes because she likes to have a record of who talked about what at these meetings.

The highlight of the afternoon is the bestowing of a career award on an old teacher of Frankie's, Judge Elwood Beale. Frankie has little interest even in this event, except that when Judge Beale is called to the dais, he is assisted by a stunning young blonde whose beauty and grace produce a quickening of Frankie's pulse. Who is she? Frankie finds the young woman an incitement to lust, fantasy, a sharp quivering in her belly. Is she so sexually bereft that she needs to respond like this to any attractive female? No, this one is something special, a rarity, tall, long-boned, a perfect face with high cheekbones, a wide mouth painted a light pink. The blonde is ravishing, a delight for the eyes. She assists Judge Beale to the podium, and then she sits on a nearby chair as if to watch over him. Who is she? Frankie only half-listens to the judge's words as he begins speaking in a slow hoarse voice. Her attention is instead fixed on the blonde, on the blonde's face, her classic beige dress, the lines of her lovely legs in beige hose, the delicate shoes with modest heels. She's past thirty but not more than thirty-five, a blooming young woman with an appearance of an intense vitality. And, as Frankie stares at her, the young woman finally turns her head to look at Frankie. Not a glance, but a look; a long look, a meeting of the eyes, a contact both electric and definite.

Oh, yes, Frankie thinks. She has a sudden desire to throw herself on the dais and find the blonde's cunt with her mouth. Oh, yes, indeed.

The judge speaks only briefly, graciously accepting

the award with an amusing story about his youth in law school. When he finishes, the attorneys in the audience applaud with gusto, happy that one of their own has been honored, happy that the dull meeting is finished at last. Frankie immediately leaves her seat and goes to the dais to greet her old teacher.

Judge Beale doesn't recognize her at first, and then his eyes turn wide and bright and he says, "Ah, Frances Hooper, how are you?"

Frankie chats with the old judge. Before long the judge turns to the blonde young woman. "Alison, meet Frances Hooper, one of my best students. Frances, this is my daughter."

Frankie's mission is accomplished, the introduction achieved. The blonde's name is Alison, and she's the judge's daughter. How marvelous.

"Hooper?" the blonde says. "I know a tennis coach named Sally Hooper."

"A distant cousin."

The blonde smiles. "How nice." More talk. Frankie helps Alison get the old judge off the dais. Other attorneys are approaching now, the judge shaking hands, nodding at old friends.

Frankie looks at Alison and asks whether Alison is an attorney. "Oh no," Alison says. "I was a bad girl and I avoided law school. I'm in advertising."

She runs a small agency specializing in fashion. Frankie is impressed, more interested than ever, almost quivering with a need to know her better.

But before long it's time to leave, and sanity requires a polite exit.

"Well, good-bye," Frankie says. Alison smiles. "Thanks for helping me with Dad."

An hour later, Frankie sits in her office in a state of distraction. She can't think of anything but the blonde, the judge's daughter, the blonde Alison Beale. Behind Frankie, the law books catch the light of the dying western sun. Her desk is huge, uncluttered because she hates a cluttered desk. The two large windows overlook the western part of the city, the sprawling avenues that go on and on to the far horizon. On most afternoons she enjoys watching the sun make its descent, the orange sky, the first lights of the city twinkling in the dusk. But this afternoon all she thinks about is Alison Beale.

At last, with a sigh, Frankie reaches for the phone book on the shelf behind her and flips the pages to find the Beales. Beale and Beale and Beale. And finally Alison Beale and two listed phone numbers, one residential and the other a downtown office. Frankie calls the office number, and she feels a wave of happiness when she is put through immediately to Alison Beale.

"I thought we might have lunch sometime," Frankie says. And on the other end of the line, Alison Beale says yes, she'd like that, she'd like that very much.

They agree on a day and a place, and when Frankie puts the phone down she looks at the instrument as if to recognize for the first time what a definite miracle it is.

Alison Beale will have lunch with her in a few days. Frankie quivers, a sudden heat rising in her belly, a sudden uncontrolled passion for a woman hardly met and hardly known. Not known at all, really. Is it merely a woman she wants? Is that it? Giddy with her success at connecting with Alison, Frankie abruptly decides on a lark. Yes, why not? Oh, my, yes, she thinks, what a lovely idea.

It's almost five o'clock when Frankie enters the lobby

of the North Michigan Avenue hotel. Valerie has already been notified not to expect Frankie home until eight or nine, and the hotel has already been contacted to provide a room for the evening. And so, when Frankie approaches the desk and gives her name, the arrangements require no more than five minutes. After that she has her key and a pleasant smile from the desk clerk as he says, "Have a nice stay, Ms. Hooper."

Upstairs in the room, Frankie calls down to order a bottle of chilled Chablis, and then she makes another call to a number outside the hotel, holding a credit card in her hand as she speaks softly into the telephone with her eyes on the window looking north along the busy boulevard. In a few moments the phone is down again, and Frankie sighs as she lies back on the bed thinking, well, it's done, so stop worrying about whether you ought to do it because you've already done it. What she feels now is a marvelous tingling anticipation. She tells herself that this is one way, at least, not to think about Alison Beale.

The wine arrives. After the hotel porter leaves, Frankie draws the drapes across the window and pours herself a glass of cool Chablis. She feels good now, much much better. More settled. The anticipation is still there—the boiling under the surface—but she has the lid on enough to keep her mind clear.

Time passes. As she finishes the second glass of wine, someone knocks on the door.

Frankie goes to the door and opens it, and there stands a thin blonde in a red dress, a string of Italian beads around her neck, a large leather shoulder bag, charcoal stockings, and black heels.

The girl smiles at Frankie. "Hi, I'm Carol." Frankie holds the door open as the girl walks past her and into the room. After Frankie closes and locks the door, she follows the girl and says, "Would you like some wine?"

"Sure, why not?" Frankie pours the wine as the girl drops her purse on one of the chairs near the window.

As she hands the glass to the girl, Frankie says, "I'm glad you could make it so quickly."

The girl smiles. "I never lose any time when they tell me it's a woman."

Frankie chuckles. As she sips the wine, she looks the blonde over from head to toe. "You're very attractive," Frankie says.

The girl smiles again, sits on one of the two easy chairs and crosses her long legs. "What would you like me to call you?"

"Frankie."

"Hi, Frankie. Gee, this wine is good. I'm glad it's wine and not something stronger. Sometimes I just drink too much."

"That's not good for you."

"I guess not. Would you like me to get more comfortable? You just tell me what you want. Suppose I take my dress off."

Frankie nods. "All right, go on and do that." Apparently happy, the blonde puts her wineglass on the table beside her chair and rises. She weaves her hips from side to side as she begins unbuttoning the row of small white buttons down the front of her dress. "I can tell we're going to have a good time," the girl says.

"How can you tell?"

"Just instinct, I guess. I just look at you and I know it. Sometimes I get these phony old bitches, and they're so dull. They don't know what they want, or if they want it, or whatever. Am I talking too much? Just tell me and I'll stop."

"No, it's all right." But Frankie has no interest in the blonde's account of her experiences. She watches the girl as she slips out of the red dress. Carol now shows a red lace bra and panty set, and a red lace garter belt with long straps to hold up her charcoal stockings. The girl does a turn to exhibit her body, and when she faces Frankie again, she giggles as she casually cups her crotch with her hand.

"Getting undressed for a woman always turns me on." Then Carol sits down again, crosses her legs, and lifts her wineglass, sips her wine, and then uncrosses her legs and leaves them open. Her crotch is revealed, still covered by the panties, but the plumpness of the mound evident.

Frankie's need is to be gruff, to emphasize the imbalance. She's paying for it, isn't she? If she wanted a romantic interlude, false as it might be, she could easily find one in a bar on Halsted. No, this is something different, an amusement requiring no commitment. And all because of Alison Beale. Because if it hadn't been for that blonde Alison, the little demons in Frankie's head would never have been allowed their voice.

"Show me the tits," Frankie says. Carol blushes, aware that Frankie is suddenly the butch she appears to be in the first place. After placing her wineglass on the table, Carol unsnaps the front of the skimpy bra and gets rid of it completely. She pulls her shoulders back to emphasize her small breasts, but she has hardly enough there to make a display. This annoys Frankie, who would rather have a girl with breasts than a girl without breasts; but then, of course, it's her own fault for not asking for it on the telephone.

Maybe Carol is aware of it. With an artful attempt to compensate by deliberately calling attention to herself, Carol takes her pinkish nipples between her thumbs and forefingers and pulls them outward. "I'm not very big in the tit department." Then she slides a hand between her legs, her fingers tugging at the crotch of her panties, and she gives Frankie a coy look. "Should I take these off?"

Frankie takes in the offering. Carol's fingers have pulled enough of the panty crotch aside to reveal part of her cunt, almost all of the left outer lip, puffy, hairless, and definitely more interesting than her breasts.

Frankie nods. Yes, she'll have a look at the cunt now. She sips her wine as Carol hurriedly raises her hips and slides the panties down her thighs and off her stocking-clad legs. For a moment, the panties are caught on a stiletto heel, but finally they're free, and Carol drops them on the table on top of her discarded bra.

Now, when the blonde opens her legs, her shaved cunt is visible, a ripe-looking fig split by the pinkish-brown stripe of the closed inner lips. Without waiting for Frankie to ask for it, Carol sensually glides her fingers down to pry apart the short wattles.

"You're making me hot," Carol says, her voice sultry. Is it feigned? Frankie has no idea. For the moment, her attention is fixed on the displayed cunt. She asked for a blonde, and a blonde is what they sent her. Now the question is how closely this blonde cunt resembles the blonde cunt of Alison Beale. Are they similar? Stupid games, Frankie thinks. She tells herself to forget about Alison for the time being and concentrate on the moment.

Frankie rises, gesturing to Carol to do the same. When Carol stands, Frankie makes another gesture with her hand and Carol smiles and slowly turns to show her ass. The buttocks are full, round, pale white, framed by the red garter belt and the red garter straps and the tops of the charcoal stockings. Frankie moves forward to place the flat of her right hand on the split between the two buttocks, her finger sliding down, curling in to find the hairless lips of the girl's vulva.

Carol makes a whimpering sound of delight as she moves her legs apart and then bends forward a bit from her waist. "Hey, I like you."

Frankie's left hand moves to Carol's belly, and then upward to close over one of Carol's small breasts. "Bend forward some more."

Carol bends. Frankie helps by pulling on the breast she holds with her hand, pulling it down until Carol is now bent forward enough so she needs to position her hands on her thighs to balance herself. About to say something, Carol suddenly moans as she feels Frankie's fingers penetrate her cunt from behind.

Frankie now shifts her body backward a bit, so she's now more directly behind Carol, her left hand still holding one of Carol's breasts while the fingers of her right hand pierce the opening of Carol's vagina. Pinching the blonde's nipple between her thumb and forefinger as she continues to hold the breast, Frankie starts fucking the blonde with the fingers of her right hand.

Carol groans. Now there is no question of artifice. The groan is definitely not feigned. The blonde hips are weaving slowly from side to side as Frankie's two fingers slide in and out of her wet opening.

"Oh, baby, fuck me," Carol says with a whimper. And for the next half hour, Frankie does exactly that, two fingers and then three fingers and then two fingers again, until her wrist is tired, her mind exhausted and she wants nothing more of the silly blonde and her swollen little cunt. Frankie sends her away without ever removing her own clothes. Later, in the hotel bathroom, Frankie masturbates in the shower with a bar of soap as she thinks of Alison Beale again.

# NINE

# **Valerie**

Valerie is preparing herself. She has the blinds open, the sunlight in the room to make it easier to see her face in the mirror as she applies the makeup. Except for the thigh-high stockings with elastic tops, she's naked, but the stockings are temporary because she hasn't yet decided to wear these or another pair. These stockings are a cool blue-gray, and she isn't certain about the color. Maybe Cleo won't like them. Maybe plain beige would be best. Cleo said, "Dress up," and so Valerie is doing that, but without any certainty that what she's doing will meet with Cleo's approval. Poor little baby, Valerie thinks. Her lipstick is a pinkish red, carefully applied to the outline of her lips, moist enough to make her lower lip shine seductively. The shade is new, chosen deliberately in accordance with Cleo's declaration that a woman's lipstick ought to be the same shade as the color of her sex lips. And so Valerie passed a serious time at the Saks cosmetics counter attempting to match the color of her petals. Not too easy, since she's never been very good with colors. She thought of taking a dozen lipstick tubes into a dressing room somewhere to make a match, but the idea seemed unworkable.

After she finishes the makeup, she preens a bit in front of the full-length mirror attached to the door of the bathroom. She stands in front of the mirror and she turns her body to look at her profile, her breasts and belly and ass and legs in the blue-gray stockings. Now she wants a pair of heels, and she hurries to closet to find her blue-gray suede sandals. Yes, they're perfect, and after she has the straps buckled she prances back to the mirror to see the full effect again, her body now lifted four inches by the high heels, the muscles in her calves more prominent, her legs more curvaceous.

After that she dresses in lace bikini panties and a lace bra sheer enough to show her nipples. Both bra and panties are blue because Cleo likes her in blue. Valerie thinks she looks better in red or black underwear; but if Cleo wants blue, Cleo gets blue. Valerie doesn't mind it; she's thrilled she has a lover who cares about the color of her underwear.

She chooses a white dress, knee-length with spaghetti shoulder straps, a tucked bodice and a flaring pleated skirt. A necklace of small white pearls and small pearl earrings complete the ensemble. You're not bad, she thinks. She tells herself she looks good today. Her face looks rested, and she has an attractive flush in her cheeks because of the excitement she feels about her date with Cleo. Then she has a sudden worry that she'll get wet thinking about Cleo, and she doesn't want that because she might lose control and masturbate, and she might get sweaty enough to ruin her makeup. No, not now, she thinks. Fearful that another moment in front of the mirror will make her too hot, she grabs a small white purse and hurries out of the apartment.

"I like the dress," Cleo says, turning her attention from the traffic to smile at Valerie.

Cleo is driving her black Trans Am, and now they're rolling west on Addison. Valerie has no idea what the destination is, a friend of Cleo's, a house somewhere, maybe an afternoon party of some kind.

Cleo extends her right hand to stroke Valerie's knee. She continues driving like that, her left hand on the wheel and her right hand on Valerie's knee. Then Cleo's fingers gather the hem of Valerie's white dress, and she pulls the dress back far enough to reveal the top of one stocking and a garter attachment.

"Blue garter belt," Cleo says with a soft laugh.

"You told me you like blue."

"That's right, doll." Cleo's fingers tickle Valerie's thigh above the top of the stocking, and then the fingers slide toward Valerie's belly, dragging the hem of the dress with them.

Valerie groans. "Cleo, someone will see us." Cleo glances down at the edge of the exposed blue panties, her fingers now finding the wetness in the crotch. "Hey, you're gushing," Cleo says with a chuckle. She tugs at the edge of the panties to release a tuft of Valerie's dark pubic hair.

Valerie groans again, closing her eyes, relinquishing any attempt to caution Cleo about passing cars or the people in the street. So what if anyone see them. People see worse these days.

Cleo has her fingers under the nylon now, her middle finger gently stroking the shaft of Valerie's clitoris, prodding it from side to side as they continue rolling west on Addison. It's not enough to make Valerie come, but it's enough to drive her crazy, and Cleo knows it.

Cleo says, "Slide forward a little."

"You'll get us in trouble, Cleo."

"Slide forward, honey." Valerie does it. She slides her hips forward on the seat, which makes it possible for Cleo to get her middle finger inside her vagina. Cleo stirs the finger around in the wetness, and then finally pulls her hand away and brings it back to her mouth to taste Valerie's syrup.

"Sweet doll." Valerie groans.

"Oh, Cleo, I love you."

"Give me the panties. Take them off and give them to me." Quivering, Valerie gets her hands underneath her dress and lifts her hips, then slides the panties down her thighs and off her legs. When she hands the wisp of blue nylon to Cleo, the firm-jawed blonde immediately brings the panties to her face to sniff the crotch.

"Valerie's little rose garden," Cleo says with a laugh. "I love it!"

They walk into a small clapboard house on a quiet residential street near Western Avenue. In the front hallway, voices can be heard from somewhere. Cleo seems to know the house well, and she leads Valerie along the hall to an open doorway and into a large living room.

Four women are in the room, sprawled in various places, on the sofa, on the chairs, one woman on the rug. As Cleo and Valerie enter the room, the four women stop talking and look up at them.

"Hey, how's it going?" Cleo says. "This is Valerie." Of the four women, two are obviously butch, one a heavyweight bruiser. The two femmes are blondes in their thirties, curled hair and heavily made-up faces and red lipstick. One of them has her blouse unbuttoned down to the waistband of her skirt, a white lace bra visible in the opening.

All the women look at Valerie, who manages a weak hello as she stands there under scrutiny during an awkward moment.

Finally the scrutiny ends and the two newcomers are welcomed, offered a drink, and told where to find it.

The heavyweight dyke goes by the name of Brady, and it appears that the house is hers. "I guess we're all here, so I'm locking the front door," Brady says. She gives Valerie a long look, her eyes lingering on Valerie's breasts, and then dropping down to glance at Valerie's shoes. This deliberately sexual look makes Valerie quiver, and she immediately turns away to find Cleo and sit beside her on the sofa.

Someone switches on the stereo, a wild song by Ina Morgan. Valerie sips her wine as she watches and listens to the others. She thinks the two femmes aren't as pretty as she is, and she's grateful for it. She hates being at a party and hardly knowing anyone, but at least she can feel confident about her looks. The two femmes could almost be sisters, except that one is much taller and probably a real blonde while the other one looks bleached. Valerie isn't certain yet whether the femmes and butches are permanently coupled. Sometimes you think it's a couple, and then it turns out it's just a casual date. Anyway, what's the difference? she thinks. For the moment, all that really concerns her is keeping her dress down because Cleo has her panties in her pocket.

The other butch is Ricky, and now Ricky says, "Hey, Doreen, how come you're not dancing?"

Doreen is the smaller blonde. She smirks as she gets to her feet. She gives Valerie a cool glance, and then she snaps her fingers and starts dancing.

Valerie is surprised because Doreen is actually good at it, a smooth dancer with a willowy body. She's wearing a tight skirt and heels, but she still manages to move with abandon to the heavy beat of the music.

Then, after a while, Cleo calls out, "Give us the mogambo."

And Ricky agrees. "Yeah, the mogambo, baby." Valerie has no idea what the mogambo is, but Doreen is smiling now as she begins unbuttoning the front of her blouse while she continues dancing. She moves her hips and legs and shoulders as she slowly undoes one button after the other.

Valerie soon understands the intention, and she feels a quickening of her pulse as she leans against Cleo's shoulder and watches the blonde. The room feels like a hothouse now, and Valerie is worried about her lack of panties, worried she'll stain her dress. Then she tells herself the hell with it and she sips more of her wine.

Doreen gets the blouse off, and Valerie is shocked when she sees the low-slung breasts captured by a bra with its tips cut away to expose the nipples. The lewd exposure of Doreen's brown nipples seems to electrify everyone, and in response Doreen sways her hips and smiles and then pulls her nipples out with her fingertips.

Luanne, the other blonde, now slides into Brady's lap and giggles as Brady squeezes one of her breasts through her dress.

Valerie trembles as she feels Cleo's hand sliding between her knees. She wants to tell Cleo to stop, but her body wants something else. With a soft moan against Cleo's shoulder, she opens her legs wider to give Cleo's hand more room.

Doreen is now dropping her skirt. She's wearing a garter belt and stockings and crotchless panties, the cutaway crotch a suitable complement to the cutaway bra, her pubic hair bulging through the open crotch like a dark forest. She tosses the skirt away and, after a mocking glance in Valerie's direction, she starts dancing again.

Cleo now turns to Valerie, and she kisses Valerie's mouth. "Remember what you promised?"

Valerie shudders. "Do they know?"

Cleo chuckles. "Sure they know. That's what the party is all about."

With a groan, Valerie closes her eyes. "Oh, Cleo, I don't know—"

"Why don't you get up and dance for us? You've got a better body than that bitch Doreen."

"I don't know if I'm up to this." But she gets up and moves forward. Brady and Ricky immediately start clapping when they see Valerie's intention. Still dancing, Doreen looks up and down at Valerie before moving aside to make room for her.

Valerie starts dancing. She moves easily to the music, aware of all the eyes on her, especially Cleo's eyes. Then she tunes out the others and concentrates on Cleo. She dances only for Cleo. She keeps her eyes on Cleo as she begins unbuttoning the front of her dress. Someone claps as she slips the spaghetti straps off her shoulders one after the other. They clap again as she pushes the dress downward past her hips. Brady curses when it becomes evident that Valerie isn't wearing panties. Valerie drops the dress completely, her dark thicket exposed at the joining of her thighs. She steps out of the dress, her legs sleek in the blue-gray stockings; and then, as she faces

Cleo, she cups a hand over her crotch as she continues dancing.

Ricky laughs, says something to Cleo, and then she gets up and starts dancing opposite Valerie. They dance facing each other, and Valerie blushes as she see Ricky's eyes drop to her mound. Valerie gasps as Ricky reaches out to touch her. She looks at Cleo, but Cleo is only smiling and nodding and telling her it's all right. Too late now, anyway. Ricky already has her middle finger hooked inside Valerie's cunt, Valerie hooked on the finger as they continue dancing together.

Before long the other women rise one after the other until all are dancing near Valerie. For the first time, Valerie notices that Luanne has her clothes off, everything stripped off except a single gold bracelet around her left wrist. Luanne seems far away as she dances, as if she's in her own dreamworld.

Brady takes Ricky's place in front of Valerie. When the massive woman extends her thick fingers to probe Valerie's cunt, Valerie closes her eyes as she humps her pelvis backward and forward. She tells herself that Cleo wants it. She's doing this for Cleo. This and what will happen later. It's what will happen later that really frightens her. She doesn't mind Brady's finger inside her cunt. The big woman is as strong as an ox, and she knows how to use her finger in there. Before long Brady pulls her finger out of Valerie's cunt. She smiles at Valerie before she licks it clean.

"Hey, Luanne, come here," Brady says, and when tall Luanne wiggles across the rug to her lover, Brady slides her hand over Luanne's ass and pushes her wet finger between Luanne's buttocks. Luanne groans and closes her eyes as she gets Brady's finger in her ass. Valerie can't see it, but she knows what's happening, and her heart pounds as she watches it.

114

Valerie lies on her back across the bed with two women on either side of her, Brady and Luanne on one side and Ricky and Doreen on the other side. Cleo stands at the side of the bed between Valerie's feet with a can of Crisco in her hands.

"Put your knees up," Cleo says. Valerie puts her knees up, keeping them well apart, her cunt now exposed completely to everyone, but especially to Cleo as she stands in front of Valerie looking down at her.

Cleo talks about the Crisco as she starts smearing it on her right hand. She says that the nice thing about Crisco is that it washes out easily. All it takes is a single douche to get all of it washed away.

Valerie listens, but she's still afraid. She's also rattled by the presence of the four other women. Brady now has a hand on one of Valerie's breasts, her thick fingers teasing the nipple. Valerie is still puzzled by the arrangement here; who belongs to whom, and why does Cleo allow her friends to touch her so much? All that fingering while they were dancing. She gets jealous each time she sees Cleo touch one of the other femmes.

Cleo now reaches down to touch Valerie's cunt with her greased hand. "Start relaxing, doll."

Her knees up, Valerie trembles as she waits for it. She wonders what Frankie would say if she saw her now. Frankie would scream. The image of Frankie screaming at her makes Valerie giggle. Cleo thinks it's because she's tickling Valerie, and the blonde immediately works another finger inside Valerie's cunt. She has four fingers in the opening now. In another moment, she folds her thumb into the other fingers and she starts the full penetration. When she gets to the knuckle hurdle, she pushes firmly. "Relax, doll."

Valerie feels it. She feel the whole hand going in, and it makes her crazy with excitement. She feels Cleo clench and unclench her fist, and it drives her wild. She looks at Cleo, and she sees Cleo smiling.

"See, I told you it was easy," Cleo says. Valerie groans, and she looks at the others watching her, watching Cleo's wrist, watching Cleo fucking her with her fist.

This is serious, Valerie thinks. This is serious fucking. Oh, my, yes.

# TEN

# **Frankie**

"I hope you like the salad," Alison says. They are sitting in the small dining room of Alison's apartment. Alison called Frankie at her office in the morning to ask whether they could have lunch in Alison's apartment instead of in a restaurant. Of course, Frankie agreed immediately, delighted by the promise of a more intimate setting.

And now Frankie is even more delighted because Alison appears so receptive to a friendship.

This is Alison's lunch, prepared by Alison, a lovely salad, fish, white wine, an elegant table set near a wide window overlooking Lake Michigan. Alison wears a becoming beige silk dress, simultaneously casual and chic. Frankie wears a tailored suit and a red string tie. The afternoon sun is brilliant on the lake, but since the windows face east, the sun is not directly in the room.

Frankie feels as though she's falling in love. She gazes at Alison's face, at the curves of Alison's breasts in the silk dress, at Alison's hands, then again at Alison's lightly painted mouth. Frankie tells herself that Alison is perfect, a stunning creature, unbelievably exciting. What a miracle to meet such a woman at a gathering of lawyers!

Frankie says, "The salad is delicious. And the view is lovely."

"Yes, the lake is pretty, isn't it?"

"I meant another view. I meant the view across the table."

Alison blushes, but it's only a slight blush, and she has no trouble meeting Frankie's eyes as she says, "Were you surprised that I suggested we have lunch here?"

"Yes, I was."

"I thought I'd like to prepare a lunch for you. I don't do it often, but I thought I'd like it."

"And do you?"

Alison laughs. "Yes, very much."

"Good."

"Now I'll ask a personal question. Do you live alone?"

"No, I'm living with someone. Her name is Valerie, and we've been together almost two years."

Alison seems unruffled, her eyes once again meeting Frankie's. "All right, I won't ask any more questions."

"Don't be silly, I don't mind it."

But Alison rises and goes to the kitchen. When she returns, she says, "Before I moved into this apartment, I lived with a woman nearly three months."

"Do you still see her?"

Alison shakes her head. "She's in Paris. She's

120

French. She was here at the consulate. No, it's finished. It was never meant to be anything, anyway. I'm telling you about it because I want you to know there was nothing before it and nothing after it. I'm not very experienced, you see."

They stand at the window. Alison faces the lake, and Frankie stands beside her with her head turned as she kisses Alison's ear. The kiss is light, grazing, indefinite. Now Frankie's left arm slides around Alison's waist, and she moves behind her to kiss the side of her neck. Alison shivers, but she does not pull away. Frankie kisses her neck again, a longer kiss, her wet lips sliding down to the soft place where Alison's neck joins her shoulder.

Now Alison shifts her body to the side as if to pull away. As she does this, she turns her head toward Frankie, and Frankie immediately kisses her mouth.

The kiss seems to freeze Alison, and her body remains motionless as their lips press together. Frankie's mouth is open, her tongue mobile, aggressive, pushing between Alison's lips as Alison gradually yields to the kiss. Frankie's hand now slides upward to gently stroke Alison's breasts through the front of her silk dress. Alison moans against Frankie's mouth, her body bending backward against the support of Frankie's left arm.

Her hand leaving Alison's breasts, Frankie slips a shoulder strap down over Alison's shoulder. She does the same to the other shoulder strap, the front of the dress falling, Frankie's fingers tugging the silk downward until the lace cups of Alison's white bra are exposed, the cups almost demi-cups, the naked upper part of each breast offered up like a ripe fruit. Frankie frees Alison's left breast completely, and she bends her head to take the full pink nipple in her mouth.

Alison makes a sound of pleasure in her throat. She lifts her head back as Frankie takes her breast. Frankie sucks at the nipple, flutters her tongue over it. At the same time, she gathers the front of Alison's silk dress with her right hand and quickly raises it, and slides her hand between Alison's thighs. The blonde moans again, and then her legs part and Frankie's fingers glide into the warm crotch of Alison's pantyhose.

Anxious to get beyond the first crisis, Frankie is insistent with her hand. Of course the reinforced nylon crotch of the pantyhose is a nuisance, but she does her best with it, her fingers rubbing everywhere over the lush vulva until she's able to find the top of the groove and then finally the stiff little promontory of Alison's clitoris. At this moment there is no time for niceties, so Frankie uses her hand to rub all of Alison's cunt without favoring any part of it, a vigorous and relentless rubbing that soon has Alison gasping as she comes against Frankie's palm.

Frankie is thrilled at the gushing wetness of Alison's cunt, the total yielding. Her hand remaining cupped over Alison's crotch, Frankie waits until the orgasm is finished before she says, "Let's go to the bedroom."

Alison opens her eyes, groaning. "Frankie, please ...."

Frankie tells Alison she wants to suck her, but Alison pleads no, she's had enough for now; it's not possible.

"That's absurd," Frankie says. But Alison insists. She's expecting a business associate.

She can't take any more now anyway. She promises to see Frankie again soon. "I promise," she says.

After a while Frankie leaves her. In the elevator, Frankie sniffs at her fingers and she almost has an orgasm as she catches Alison's scent.

Midnight. Frankie lies in the bed in the dark. She has her knees up under the sheet, her eyes open, as she peers through the darkness at the ceiling. Her body feels sweaty, her pubic hair damp. Valerie is asleep beside her, turned on her side, her back to Frankie.

Frankie thinks about Alison. She feels a sudden burst of sexual heat in her belly as she remembers what happened with Alison in Alison's living room. She recalls the feel of Alison's breasts in her hands, the spongy stiffness of Alison's nipples in her mouth. Dropping her knees, Frankie crosses her legs and flexes her thigh muscles to apply pressure against her cunt. No, it's no good. She raises her knees again, shifting her buttocks on the bed.

The most exciting memory is the memory of Alison's cunt responding to her fingers. And Alison's long blonde eyelashes as she kept her eyes closed. Frankie remembers the sweetness of her victory as she watched Alison come, as she watched Alison's lips open, Alison exposed.

The memories have now aroused Frankie to an unbearable restlessness. She continues to evoke erotic images as she slides a hand between her legs. But no matter how vulnerable Alison seemed at the moment of her orgasm, she is still an enigma to Frankie, a mystery unfathomed.

Frankie finds her clitoris and rubs it slowly. She stifles a soft groan as Valerie continues sleeping beside her. The hot desire in Frankie's belly demands its due. She rubs her clitoris with her fingers, applying more pressure as the orgasm approaches.

You're lost, she thinks. She understands that she hasn't a glimmer of reality about Alison. Her mind is filled with Alison, filled to a point of bursting. All she can think of is Alison's wet cunt.

Frankie comes. She does her best to control the shaking of her body as a fury of passion overwhelms her.

Valerie sleeps on.

Frankie is in the bathtub. It's nine o'clock in the evening, and she's having a bath after a long day at court. Her body is extended, soaking in the warm water. Earlier, Valerie seemed mystified by Frankie's fatigue and suggested that Frankie might be sick. But Frankie replied that she was only tired.

At this moment, Frankie feels that the bathroom is a refuge. Poor Valerie. How awful it must be to live with me, Frankie thinks. Does Valerie understand anything at all about her? What she thinks, why she does certain things. Frankie strokes her body under the water, the firm flesh of her thighs. She looks at her hands, at the slender fingers that she wishes were stronger. She has always wanted to be physically strong.

The air in the bathroom is filled with moisture, the light in the ceiling scintillating through the mist. Frankie wipes away the sweat that has gathered on the bridge of her nose. She has a sudden memory of Alison's ass in that silk dress she wore when they had lunch, Alison's buttocks shimmering under the silk as she walked back and forth between the kitchen and the dining room. Frankie is annoyed because so little really happened that day, not as much as she wanted, not as much as she'd imagined. She'd had hot fantasies about the first time with Alison, searing images of herself doing things to Alison, kissing her everywhere, her cunt, her clitoris, her ass, rimming her little anus with the tip of her tongue and hearing Alison cry out with pleasure.

Frankie looks at her arms now, wondering

whether she ought to add more bath oil to the water. She wipes her chin with a wet cloth. What fascinates her about Alison is the hunt, the schemed seduction of a woman as intelligent as herself. Oh, God, how juicy she was! Frankie quivers as she remembers Alison's wet sex gushing on her fingertips.

Frankie hears a knock on the bathroom door, and then Valerie's voice. "Is it all right if I come in?"

Frankie says yes, and the door opens and Valerie enters the bathroom. "Aren't you wilting?" Valerie says.

"No, I like it this way." Valerie sniffs at the perfumed oil in the bath. She wears a blue robe that Frankie thinks would look better on a blonde. But she loves Valerie; she does love her. A cherished love. She's always happy to see Valerie's mouth spread in an open smile. She watches Valerie as she turns to look at herself in the mirror over the bathroom sink. The blue robe is thin enough to reveal the shape of Valerie's buttocks, and Frankie feels a tingling in her cunt as she remembers their last lovemaking when Valerie was particularly responsive, her clitoris like a stiff little pod between Frankie's lips.

Without turning from the mirror, Valerie says, "Would you like me to wash your back?"

Frankie feels a sudden desire for her. "Sure, why not?" Valerie's turns and smiles, her happiness evident, her pretty face reminding Frankie how perfect Valerie is for her sometimes. So feminine. It was Valerie's easy femininity that attracted Frankie so strongly in the beginning, her delight in the feminine trappings, garter belts, makeup, endless jewelry. When they met, Frankie thought Valerie a lovely young woman with a sweet heart, breasts like ripe mangoes in her hands.

Their eyes meet and Valerie blushes, her lower lip pouting seductively. "I'll take my robe off so I won't get it wet."

Frankie nods. She wants Valerie more than ever now, her fingers itching for it as she watches Valerie pull her hair back before slipping out of her blue robe.

Under the robe, Valerie is quite naked. For a moment she stands there without moving as if she's on the edge of a chasm between them. Then, finally, she steps forward to approach the tub where Frankie is half-immersed in the soapy water.

Frankie's eyes are riveted on Valerie's gently bobbing breasts. She feels a great desire to take one of the tender nipples in her mouth and bite it until Valerie moans.

Now Frankie sits up in the water as Valerie crouches beside the tub to wash her back. As Valerie slides the soap over Frankie's shoulders, Frankie drops her right arm over the side of the tub and curls it around Valerie's thigh to fondle her ass.

Valerie giggles. "You'll make me drop the soap."

"Darling, this was your idea." Frankie wants her in bed, but that can wait until later. She slides her hand down over Valerie's ass to find Valerie's cunt with her fingers. From long habit, she knows exactly how Valerie needs to be opened this way, how to get the proper angle from the rear to make penetration into the tight vaginal canal easy.

Valerie groans. Her eyes closed, she no longer bothers moving the soap over Frankie's back.

"Stand up," Frankie says. "It'll be easier when you're standing."

Valerie rises. Her face flushed, she stands with her legs apart as Frankie penetrates her vagina again. This time Frankie has her thumb on Valerie's clitoris, the ball of her thumb massaging the pearl as her fingers churn in the wet opening.

Valerie groans. "Oh, Frankie!" As the orgasm approaches, she begins moving her hips, humping her pelvis at Frankie's hand.

Frankie gazes up at Valerie's face, watching the climax, watching Valerie's pleasure. "Sweet pet," Frankie says. She keeps her fingers working, thrusting, churning in the hot opening.

# ELEVEN

# **Frankie**

Frankie waits three days before she telephones Alison. The blonde's voice is cool, uncommitted. "I don't know about this afternoon."

Frankie says, "What about tomorrow?"

"I don't know."

"All right, forget it. I'm getting the picture."

"No, this afternoon is all right."

"Are you sure?" Alison says yes, she's sure, and they agree Frankie will visit her at three o'clock.

After Frankie hangs up the phone, she sits in her office simmering with expectation, memories of her hands on Alison's body. Maybe it's a mirage. Maybe none of it is real. Does that lovely blonde really want her? Frankie slides a hand under her gray flannel skirt to hold her crotch through her pantyhose. She can feel the dampness, the heat of her cunt. Alison is truly a miracle, a vision who suddenly walked into

her life, a ripe fantasy. So ripe. Frankie tells herself
she has never seen anyone so ripe for it. She has
work on her desk, but now, after talking to Alison,
she's unable to concentrate. She wants Alison in her
arms, the fabric of Alison's dress rubbing against her
skin, Alison's firm ass beneath her hands. That
blonde skin. Frankie quivers as she remembers the
softness of Alison's breasts, the feel of Alison's wet
cunt. She remembers Alison's slender hips, the soft
curves, the pink shells of Alison's ears. Christ, you're
in love, Frankie thinks. She rises from the swivel
chair and walks to the wall between the two windows, where a small mirror is centered on the wall.
Her face looks flushed. Is it Alison, or is the room
too warm? She wishes she had on a real suit instead
of this gray tailored hybrid. How nice it would be to
go to Alison in drag. The idea amuses Frankie.

With a view of the lake in front of them, Frankie kisses Alison.

They stand at the window in Alison's living room,
Alison facing the lake, but her head turned to accept
Frankie's kiss. Then Alison pulls away and smiles.
"You ought see the view here at night. When the
moon is full."

"All right, I'll stay this evening."

Alison laughs softly. "No, you can't, I'm going out
this evening. Anyhow, I don't think there's a full
moon until the end of the month."

Frankie imagines Alison as a scamp when she was a
girl, blonde Alison mischievous and laughing. But the
present moment has more impact. Frankie kisses her
again, this time her tongue more insistent as it pushes
between Alison's lips to find her teeth. Is she wet?
Frankie wants to feel the moisture with her fingertips,
but she restrains herself. No savage lust this time. She

wants more than last time, a more definite possession. She strokes Alison's breasts through her blouse, remembering how she nursed on Alison's nipples. The light in the living room is so bright because of the wide windows overlooking the vast lake. And here, in this apartment, two women stand in their own special world. She wants to saturate herself with Alison, feast on Alison while Alison's nerves vibrate with happiness. She kisses Alison's lips again. As Alison turns her body, Frankie hears the rustling of nylon. She drops a hand to Alison's belly, feeling an imperative need to ravish her. Alison protests with a soft laugh, but Frankie's hand is already beneath the linen skirt, her fingers already stroking the puffy blonde cunt through the nylon crotch of her pantyhose.

"We'll cause a crash on the Outer Drive," Alison says, laughing again as she attempts to pull away.

Yes, maybe someone in a car on the expressway down there will look up and see two women at a window, one woman with her hand beneath the other woman's skirt. Alison wants to pull away, but Frankie prevents it. Frankie holds her in place, her left arm wrapped around Alison's narrow pliant waist as her right hand does its work between Alison's legs. Alison closes her eyes, her hips moving, a delicate flush beginning to suffuse her face as the volcano nears eruption. Frankie's fingers are relentless, her middle finger extending underneath to rub the nylon protecting Alison's sweet little anus. Does she feel it? What a vision she must be without clothes.

Frankie imagines Alison naked, her pink nipples erected, her lovely virtuous face twisted by passion. She kisses Alison again, rubbing her cunt with the heel of her palm. It's a violation, a possession by her fingers. Pity she lacks another hand to take those delicious breasts. If only she could pinch Alison's nipples at the same time. Instead she bends her head to kiss Alison's throat. She imagines she can feel Alison's clitoris against her palm, and she rubs it with more vigor. Certainly the wetness is there, the syrup seeping through the nylon into Frankie's sliding hand. Now she drops her left hand, and she gets it under Alison's skirt in the rear to fondle Alison's buttocks through her pantyhose.

Alison groans, her thighs buckling. "Please ..."

"Let's go to the bedroom."

Alison groans again. "Yes."

The bedroom is decorated in pink. Frankie is astounded because she expected something different; but it's all pink, the walls pink, the bedspread pink satin, the lamp shades of pink silk. A pink room. Frankie looks at the pink bed and imagines Alison writhing on it, her legs shaking in an ecstatic release, her ripe breasts jiggling. Is Alison always on this bed alone?

Frankie kisses Alison and starts undressing her. Alison remains passive, pliant, with a look of faint amusement as she watches Frankie's hands working to get her clothes off.

"You're very forceful," Alison says.

"Don't you like it?"

Alison laughs. "I'm not answering that."

"What sort of girl were you? Were you rebellious?"

"Yes, very."

"I thought so." Frankie's hands tremble as she unhooks Alison's brassiere.

The blonde's breasts are full, heavy enough to show a slight droop, the stiffness of the pink nipples quite evident. With deliberate restraint, Frankie does no more than rub a fingertip over one of the turgid points. "You're beautiful."

Alison laughs. "My breasts?"

"All of you."

"When I was a girl, I was always afraid my breasts would be too small. Now I'm sorry they aren't."

"No, they're perfect."

"My swinging tits."

Frankie smiles. "Quite perfect."

"You make me feel nasty when you look at me like that."

"Then I won't look, I'll just finish undressing you." Frankie is thrilled. Having Alison gradually become naked like this is a delightful treat. Alison supports herself with a hand on Frankie's shoulder as Frankie tugs her pantyhose down her thighs and off her feet. The closeness of the blonde's belly tantalizes Frankie, and her excitement becomes intense as she imagines she can smell Alison's heat, smell her sweet cunt hidden by those soft blonde curls.

When Frankie rises again, she whispers in Alison's ear, "I'm going to suck you dry."

Alison shudders. "Tell me more."

"On the bed, girl." With a moan of passion, Alison throws herself onto the bed. She rolls her naked body from side to side, and then finally she settles on her back with her legs open. "I like what you do to me."

Her eyes on Alison's blonde cunt, Frankie quickly drops her clothes. When she's down to her underpants, she climbs onto the bed and immediately drops her head to run her tongue over Alison's belly. Alison moans, raises her knees, and opens her thighs in a definite invitation. Frankie's tongue leaves a wet trail of saliva as she slides her mouth down into the blonde bush. When she glances up at Alison's face, she finds Alison watching her, Alison's blue eyes fixed on her mouth, Alison waiting.

Returning her attention to the pink flower directly

under her chin, Frankie extends her tongue for the first touch. Alison groans, raising her knees farther and holding them up with her hands. "Don't tease me."

That's what they all say, Frankie thinks. Don't tease me. But they love it anyway. Frankie blows her warm breath on Alison's open cunt, grazing the flesh with her mouth, teasing her. She flutters her tongue along the outer lips, up and down, inside the wet socket and then up to the pink little clit. Her own cunt tingles. She slides her hands under Alison's ass and she lifts the lower part of Alison's body to feast on her. Alison groans, her mouth open, her neck craned as she looks down to watch Frankie's mouth take possession of her cunt. When Alison comes, it's like a fine dessert for Frankie, a sweet cake spiked with brandy, the juices gushing out thick enough to be a definite turn-on. Oh, how she adores a gushing pussy!

Frankie lies on her back. She still wears her Jockey underpants, the cotton crotch soaked by her leaking cunt. She keeps her legs closed, listening to Alison as Alison talks about her college days at Northwestern. Rich man's daughter at a rich girl's school. Frankie turns on her side to watch the shadows fall across Alison's breasts. She understands Alison better now. Alison likes to maintain decorum. Alison is a woman who adored ruffles as a ten-year-old. Alison favors the luster of the upper class. Frankie is surprised that the old judge is so rich, but apparently he has millions. Property everywhere. She wants Alison again. She wants to lunge at her, take her forcefully, but instead she tells Alison to come on top of her. "On my face," Frankie says.

Alison evidently likes the idea. She climbs over

Frankie, straddles her, and shifts forward to get her hands on the headboard. The blonde settles in, squatting over Frankie's face, her cunt lubricating heavily again.

"Is this all right?"

Frankie pulls her down. She wants her nose in that valley of love. She runs her hands over Alison's buttocks. The blonde's cunt is open like a pink conch. Maybe she ought to press her ear to it and listen for the sea. Does Alison understand how much she adores her? Her tongue extended, Frankie sips at the liquid flowing out of Alison's source. The fountain has a good yield, and she has no qualms about sucking everything. Sometimes she dislikes the subservience implied by this position, but not with Alison. The blonde has a certain quality that makes the presence of her cunt on Frankie's face seem appropriate. Frankie now wishes that Alison had worn stockings, sheer nylons that would rub against her skin as she sucks the blonde's cunt. Dear God, what a lovely pussy she has, the lips pouting, the interior seeming to quake each time Frankie's tongue touches a sensitive place.

Frankie uses her tongue to polish the long groove, strong, efficient lapping everywhere. Alison's cunt seems to vibrate in response to the ardent attention. In a deliberate attempt to be provocative, Frankie nibbles with her teeth. She tugs at the blonde pubic hair. She slides her fingers into the crack between Alison's buttocks and she teases the blonde's anus with a wet fingertip. When Alison feels the fingertip she moans, the sound causing Frankie to push the finger at the tight orifice until she is able to slip it inside to the first knuckle. Enough for now. She yearns for the cunt. She glances up at Alison's face, but the blonde's eyes are closed. She sucks at the flowing juices as she slowly works her finger in and out of Alison's rectum. When Alison comes, her body suddenly jerks forward. She moans and posts, bobbing up and down on Frankie's mouth as Frankie drills her finger more firmly inside her ass.

"I think you've been ignoring me," Marcia says. They sit in a booth at lunch in a downtown restaurant.

Frankie thinks the food is rotten. She's annoyed that she allowed herself to be coaxed into this lunch with Marcia. Can't Marcia accept the fact that it's over? But Marcia still looks interesting, that lovely chunky body and those full calves in the dark stockings. Frankie remembers how Marcia quivers when her belly is stroked. She's a pet, really. She'd like to have her on a beach somewhere, take her on the sand while they listen to the surf. Why does she have such a penchant for women like this one?

Marcia says, "You're not even listening to me."

"What did you say"

"I said, 'I think you've been ignoring me.'"

"Yes, maybe it's true. I've been awfully busy."

Marcia pouts. "Is that all it is? I hope it's nothing more than that. I hope you're not going to dump me. I hate being dumped."

Frankie wonders how she can dump Marcia when they've never had a real relationship.

"You know I'm living with someone."

Marcia nods. "But that doesn't mean you have to dump me."

"I'm not dumping you."

"I'd like to suck you off right this moment. Maybe I could get under the table and do it."

"Marcia, please...."

Marcia giggles. "If the waiter hears me, you'll never be able to come here again."

"Then don't talk so loud." "You know what I don't like about most dykes? They're too serious. You're too fucking serious, Frankie."

Frankie doesn't bother to answer. It's no good. She thinks of Alison. She has Valerie at home and Marcia here in the restaurant, but all she wants to think about is Alison. Only Alison represents something positive in her life. Everyone she knows seems so trivial compared to Alison.

She wants Alison.

# TWELVE

# **Valerie**

Valerie meets Brady and another woman on Broadway. The sun is hot enough to bring the sweat out on their foreheads. The sun makes Valerie regret that she isn't more careful with her makeup. She likes to keep her appearance intact. She hates the feeling of vulnerability when the sun makes her wilt. When she looks at Brady, Valerie remembers how it was with Brady and Cleo and the others that time in Brady's house. She remembers Brady's hands on her ass, and it makes her quiver. Brady's huge breasts jut outward like two mountains. Her silhouette would not show a straight line anywhere. Does she remember that party? When their eyes meet, Valerie understands that Brady remembers everything.

Brady's friend calls herself Dell. She's different, less aggressive than Brady, more thoughtful. The way she looks at Valerie makes it seem as though she's trying to hypnotize her. At moments Valerie feels that she's approaching the danger zone of getting turned on. She can feel the itch, her clitoris engorged, a definite throbbing at intervals. She wonders what will happen, what the risk will be. She does not want to incite Cleo into one of her crazy jealousies. But when Brady suggests that they all go to the nearest girl-bar to drink and talk, Valerie agrees.

Walking into the bar is like stepping through a veil separating one world from another world. They take a booth and order a pitcher of beer. Brady drinks the beer and then she wipes the foam off her lips with her fingers. She looks at Valerie and says, "I like your dress."

Valerie says, "Thank you," wondering whether Brady is coming on to her. She likes the taste of the beer. She feels a surge of pleasure at not being alone this afternoon.

Brady says, "Cleo told me you're living with someone."

Valerie nods. "Yes, I am living with someone."

Brady chuckles. "Getting enough?" Valerie blushes and says nothing. She avoids their eyes, looking at the empty bar and then at her beer glass. She wonders what they think of her. Poor little femme not getting enough. She feels her breasts swelling in her bra. She has a sudden fantasy that she's on a beach, and Brady and Dell are tearing her dress off, delighting her with their hands. She imagines Dell's hands tickling the hollows, tickling between her legs as the hot sun beats down on them. She imagines the petals of her cunt opening like a hot greedy flower to their fingers.

After a while, Brady rises. "I've got some business downtown. You two have fun."

Valerie is stunned. Brady's departure is unexpected, and after she leaves the bar, Valerie feels uncomfortable with Dell because she hardly knows her.

But Dell is soft and easy—at least softer than Brady—and after a while Valerie feels more relaxed, happy with Dell because she's different, and variety is always welcome. Dell, in fact, seems a little piqued that Brady ran off like that. Brady is one of those women who always leave uncertainty behind them, like a big, fast ship rocking the small boats as it passes them. Dell nurtures this new friendship with Valerie, speaking softly, smiling, getting Valerie to understand that she finds her appealing.

"Lean forward," Dell says.

Puzzled, Valerie asks why. "What for?"

"Come on, do it. Just do it for me." When Dell looks down at Valerie's breasts, Valerie understands. She blushes and she leans forward, her blouse billowing out to make it easy for Dell to look down the neckline at her breasts.

"Sexy," Dell says with a soft laugh. "Sexy tits in a lace bra. Brady told me you had your brains fucked out at that party."

Valerie's face is red. "It's not fair to talk about people like that."

"Hell, what's the harm? Who cares? You're too pretty to care about that. Do you like me?"

Uncertain, Valerie looks at her. Dell is beefy, pushing forty, but she has a soft face and nice eyes. "Sure," Valerie says.

"I've got some toys. I'm getting hot thinking about doing you with a strap-on. How about it?"

Valerie quivers. "I don't know."

"It's boring sitting here. Let's go to my place and get comfortable, okay?"

When Dell rises, Valerie rises with her. The possibility of being abandoned in the bar is intolerable.

Dell has more grace than Brady or Cleo. She treats Valerie with care, helping her into the taxi, then helping her out of the taxi. On the stairs walking up to Dell's apartment in a small six-flat building, Dell puts a hand on Valerie's ass and keeps it there as Valerie climbs the steps in front of her. Valerie feels the strong fingers through the layers of clothing. She likes the idea that Dell wants her, wondering what Dell will do in bed. Dell makes a joke about how difficult it is to walk behind a pretty ass, and Valerie laughs as they climb the stairs.

Inside her apartment, Dell opens a window to get some air into the place. The living room is a mess, old magazines and newspapers everywhere, a food tray perched on top of the TV set. Dell brings some cold beer out of the kitchen, and after that they sit on the sofa and Dell starts groping Valerie, kissing her and fondling her breasts through her blouse. When Dell starts unbuttoning the front of her blouse, Valerie leans back with a sigh of surrender.

"Let's have a look," Dell says. She gets the blouse unbuttoned; but instead of unhooking the front of Valerie's bra, she deftly scoops Valerie's breasts out of the cups and bends her head to suck one of the nipples.

Valerie groans as she looks down at Dell's head. She can see the gray hair mixed with the red, the pink shell of one of Dell's ears. She feels wanton, totally vulnerable, willing to do anything Dell wants. She imagines a smell of womanhood in the room, a smell of ripe cunt. Maybe it's her own smell. Dell excites her because she has a definite sensuality in the way she moves and talks. Dell finishes sucking one nipple and moves to the other one. Her hand now slides between Valerie's legs and under her skirt to find her panty-covered crotch. Valerie opens her thighs as Dell's fingers lightly stroke her puffed lips through the nylon of her panties.

Dell pulls her mouth away from Valerie's breast, leaving the nipple stiff and glistening with her saliva. "What's Cleo like in bed?"

Valerie is amused. "You don't want to talk about that."

"Sure I do. Does she fuck you with a dick?"

Valerie quivers as she feels Dell's fingers pinching her labia. "No, never." She has an urge to guide the fingers inside her cunt at once, get Dell to take her immediately. She feels herself gushing, damp in the crotch. Would Cleo care about sharing her with Dell? Valerie has no qualms about opening her thighs to Dell. She slumps further on the sofa, quivers, opens her thighs wider, and looks at Dell through half-closed eyes. "I like you better than Brady."

Dell chuckles. "You do? Come on, let's get the blouse and skirt off. I'm dying to look at you."

Before long Dell has Valerie stripped down to her heels and nylons. She kisses Valerie, pushes her thick tongue inside Valerie's mouth as she strokes Valerie's thighs and tells her how much she wants to fuck her. Valerie imagines Dell lunging at her with a dildo. She knows what it's like; she had it during the wild days before she met Frankie, from the butches in the bars. Dell gets her to stand now, and Valerie thinks she can definitely smell herself, the scent of her cunt, her juices oozing between her legs.

She wonders what sort of game Dell has in mind. The air in the room is hot and damp, and she can feel the sweat between her naked breasts as Dell kisses her again. Dell kisses her mouth and chin and then her breasts. The older woman fondles Valerie's ass, whispering in her ear how pretty she is in the stockings and heels, while at the same time her fingers slide into the crack between Valerie's buttocks and one finger gently tickles Valerie's anus. Valerie trembles, hoping that Dell won't want her there—at least, not with a dildo. She has a sudden memory of Cleo taking her ass with her fingers, Cleo teasing her because she came so hard. Dell hugs her, binding her body close with her strong arms, a ray of sunlight appearing to sparkle as Valerie presses against Dell to feel the soft pillows of Dell's big breasts under her shirt.

Laughing, Dell says, "You're dripping, honey. You're hungry for it." She makes Valerie turn around and bend forward with her hands on the back of a chair. Dell stands behind her, kissing her neck and then sliding her hand between her thighs to get at her crotch. Valerie groans as she moves her legs farther apart. She feels Dell's hand down there, the strong fingers pinching and then spreading her labia. Valerie has a sudden fantasy of being fucked in a meadow by a woman wearing black leather. The idea is so unexpected that she giggles, which makes Dell think her fingers are doing it. Dell chuckles as she rubs between the lips of Valerie's cunt and inside the crack of her ass at the same time. She kisses Valerie's neck again, nibbling at her skin and then whispering in Valerie's ear, "If you'll pull your cheeks open, I'll rim you."

Valerie shudders. She lowers her shoulders to the upholstered back of the chair. Then she reaches behind with her hands to pull her buttocks apart. In a moment she feels Dell's hot breath on her ass, and then inside the crack and on her anus. A whimper of delight comes out of Valerie's throat at the first touch of Dell's wet tongue. She loves it. She loves to be treated this way, to be made love to as though she's a hot- house flower. She loves having a butch's tongue tickling and licking her ass with such artfulness that she's almost ready to come.

Dell rises. She gets her hand between Valerie's legs again, and this time she takes her with three fingers. Valerie groans, pushing her ass back to get more, anxious now to have an orgasm after all that teasing of her anus. Dell's fucking is lavish, extremely sensual, her knuckles ravaging Valerie's clitoris with each thrust of her strong fingers. Valerie comes hard, but Dell keeps fucking her until she comes again. After that Dell makes Valerie straighten up, and she kisses her. She brings her juice-coated fingers to her mouth and sucks them clean as Valerie watches her and trembles with excitement. Valerie is overcome, her mind drugged with the intense sex. She's ready for anything now, and when Dell says she'll be right back, Valerie knows what to expect and wants it desperately.

"If you want beer, it's in the fridge," Dell says.

"Okay."

The older woman playfully pinches one of Valerie's nipples and then saunters away. Valerie leaves the living room and walks into the kitchen to find a beer in the refrigerator. The kitchen window shade is up—the window facing the adjacent building—and Valerie giggles as she remembers she's wearing only stockings and heels. She hurries back to the living room, and stands near the stereo, sipping beer out of the can and slowly swaying her hips to the beat of the music.

When Dell returns, she's half-undressed, stripped to the waist with her big breasts swinging free and a long, thick dildo sticking out of the open fly of her jeans. "Here I am with my dick," Dell says with a laugh, curling her hand around the shaft of the dildo and stroking it lewdly from the tip down to the base.

Valerie blushes as she gazes at the dildo. The color is more pink than natural, and the length and thickness large enough to make the toy a bit frightening. What turns her on more than the dildo are Dell's big breasts. The brown nipples are huge, each breast like a beach ball capped with a dark moon. Dell notices Valerie's gaze, and she smiles as she releases the dildo to lift her breasts with her right forearm. "You want to suck one of these, honey? Come on, don't be bashful."

Mesmerized by the heavy breasts, Valerie moves forward to bend her head and take one of the tits in her mouth as Dell holds it up to her mouth. Dell sighs as she feels Valerie nibbling and sucking at her fat nipple. "That's good, angel. That's very good."

The sucking of Dell's big breast brings an intense heat to Valerie's cunt, the juices streaming down to the tops of her stockings. She suctions the nipple between her lips, attempting to pull it outward. She remembers a girl in college, a wild-eyed dyke with enormous breasts whose favorite game was to offer a breast to anyone at the slightest provocation. In fact, Valerie accepted the offer at a party and thus confirmed her inner yearning to be a lesbian.

Now, when she pulls her mouth away from Dell's breast, Dell smiles at her as she undulates her hips. "Go down on it, honey. Get my dick in your mouth and suck it."

Valerie blushes, remembering a nasty interlude with two motorcycle girls who made her do the same thing, except in that case one of them had a knife at her throat and she was so frightened that she wet her pants.

She drops to a crouch now, squatting in front of Dell, holding onto the denim covering Dell's big thighs as she tilts forward to take the pink dildo between her lips. The taste isn't at all rubbery—more neutral than she expected—and as she holds her head still, Dell chuckles and shoves her hips forward to bury half the length of the dildo in Valerie's mouth. "Is that too much, honey? You've got such a gorgeous mouth."

Valerie feels the excitement in her cunt as she sucks the pliable plastic dildo. She likes this kind much better than one of those hard vibrators. She likes the feel of it in her mouth, like a huge pacifier, the surface with an almost velvet texture. She smells patchouli, but she can't imagine where it's coming from. She hears Dell's heavy breathing, and when she looks up, she whimpers with lust at the sight of Dell's pendulous breasts hanging over her head. Nothing ventured, nothing gained, Valerie thinks. Is Dell the answer to her problems? Dell certainly seems more interested in giving her pleasure than Cleo does. Cleo is selfish, always prolonging the satisfaction of her own needs, never caring when Valerie complains about Cleo's fingers hurting her rectum. What Cleo likes is having Valerie's head squeezed between her muscular thighs, Valerie's head squeezed so hard she sometimes thinks she'll die that way.

Dell finally takes Valerie into the bedroom. She makes Valerie lie on her bed on her back with her knees up and apart to show her cunt. Dell talks about it, telling Valerie how pretty it is, telling Valerie how much she likes the way the hair is trimmed, and how the triangle is so perfect that it makes her salivate. Of course it's all nonsense, but Valerie loves it anyway. She adores it when a woman looks at her cunt and tells her how pretty it is. She holds her knees back with her hands, aware how exposed she is, aware of Dell's eyes on her cunt and anus. She wishes Dell would dive down and get her nose in it, polish her clit with that strong nose, but instead Dell lets her hold her legs like that as she continues feasting her eyes.

"Show me the hole," Dell says. Valerie blushes but she does it. She slides her hands down and uses her fingers, pulling her cunt apart to reveal the mouth of her vagina. Dell stares at it, smiling, her face flushed, one hand slowly stroking the dildo that protrudes from her fly.

In a moment, Dell climbs onto the bed, and the main event begins. Kneeling between Valerie's thighs, she hoists Valerie's legs over her shoulders and gets busy guiding the dildo into Valerie's wet tunnel. Valerie groans as it goes in. She keeps her eyes closed and focuses on the feel of it. A shudder passes through her body as she feels one of Dell's fingers working its way inside her anus. She hears Dell whispering at her, sweet words of encouragement—much more romantic, really, than what she gets when Cleo fucks her. The dildo feels so good in her cunt, she prays it will never stop. Her cunt is running wet, the lubrication making everything so deliciously slippery. Dell keeps that finger in her backside, screwing it in and out slowly as she continues thrusting with the dildo. When Valerie cries out, Dell starts slamming it in there to make the orgasm more intense. "Geronimo," Dell says, and Valerie screams as she comes again on the sliding prick.

# THIRTEEN

# **Frankie**

Frankie sits on a chair in Alison's bedroom. Alison is on the bed, her body wrapped in a robe, lying on her side as she idly turns the pages of a fashion magazine. Relaxed on the chair, Frankie watches Alison, her eyes on Alison's legs revealed by the askew robe, the nylon-clad ankles, the elegant high-heeled slippers that make her feet look so enchanting.

Now Alison puts the magazine away and rises from the bed. She sighs, fluffs her blonde hair, and walks over to the dressing table. Is she annoyed at something? Frankie can't imagine what it is. She always does her best to keep Alison pacified. The problem is that Alison is often too sophisticated, too difficult to please. Frankie finds it difficult to predict from one time to the next what Alison might want. The affair has a certain breathless pace—a pace determined by Alison and not by Frankie.

Alison removes her robe. Frankie feels a sudden bubble of lust forming in her belly as she looks at Alison, who is now wearing only beige stockings with elastic tops and the high heels. Alison has a definite penchant to tease. Avoiding Frankie's eyes, she stands at the dressing table toying with her bare breasts, her fingers circling the globes as though to measure them. What a pet she is. The silk panties are mauve. Her legs look so delicious in sheer nylon, her thighs firm above the dark tops of the stockings. She pulls at her nipples with her fingertips, uninhibited, playing with her body as though Frankie isn't there. Frankie has a sudden desire to touch her, and now she rises to approach Alison. For a moment they stand close without contact, Alison turning to look at Frankie, her eyes amused. On the wall behind Alison is a small oil painting of a white moon over a blue lake.

Alison says, "Why don't you undress? I never get to look at you."

Of course it's not true. She has looked at Frankie's body often enough. But Frankie doesn't argue. She turns away and she starts undressing, removing each item of her clothing with deliberate care; the suit jacket, the string tie, the white blouse, the tailored skirt. She slips her feet out of her flat shoes and she quickly gets rid of her pantyhose. Now she wears only maroon androgynous underpants. Her nipples are stiff, the areolas contracted around the dark points. When she looks at Alison, she sees the interest in Alison's eyes. What does she want? Frankie thinks. She's never comfortable being naked with a femme. She has a sudden fear that Alison will send her away. Dear god, what a wrenching beauty she is!

She imagines Alison yielding to her. She wonders whether she ought to remove her underpants, and she decides to keep wearing them. Her cunt is leaking into the crotch, and she's certain that if she opens her legs, the stain will be visible. Does Alison appreciate that? Alison is looking at Frankie, but her interest is directed at Frankie's almost-nonexistent breasts rather than at her crotch. Frankie is uneasy under Alison's gaze. She pretends to arrange her clothing on the chair, and as she does this, she willfully contracts her buttocks to produce a tingling stab of pleasure in her anus, an absurd moment that makes her want to giggle like a silly girl. Does Alison understand anything? Frankie finishes adjusting her clothing on the chair; and now, with a twinge of annoyance, she quickly peels her underpants off and tosses them onto the pile of clothes without looking at the crotch to inspect the wetness.

She faces Alison. They stand about six feet apart, Alison's right hand now raised to position her fingers in the valley between her breasts. Frankie hesitates a moment, and then she says, "Do you have any skin lotion I can use? My arms are dry."

Alison finds the plastic bottle on the dressing table and hands it to Frankie, who turns away from Alison as she squeezes out some lotion onto her palm and then rubs it into her forearm. Frankie guesses that Alison is now looking at her ass, but she'd rather have her ass looked at than the rest of her. Her technique has always been to avoid attention to her body, a ridiculous idea since women always like the way she looks.

As if reading Frankie's mind, Alison says, "I like your body."

Frankie quivers, aware of a gush of juice between her legs. Now she's wondering what to do with Alison, or what Alison will want from her. Sometimes, like now, Alison likes to extend the foreplay a long time

157

before they get down to the real fucking. Unfortunately, it's the fucking that Frankie likes best, the hard, deliberate fucking of Alison's lovely body. She quivers as she recalls probing Alison's openings with her fingers.

Unexpectedly, Alison moves closer to Frankie and she strokes one of Frankie's arms. "Are you still working out?"

Frankie nods. "It's a good health club. I could take you in as a guest sometime."

Alison smiles. "I wouldn't last five minutes in one of those places."

"But everyone needs exercise." Alison seems fascinated by Frankie's muscular arms. Frankie gazes at Alison's breasts and she feels an urge to run her tongue over the luscious tips. She's hot now. She'd like her saliva dripping on those fruity tits. She quivers as Alison's hand slides across her chest, the blonde's fingers playfully pinching one of Frankie's turgid nipples.

"Anyway, I do like your body," Alison says. "Let's get on the bed." Alison laughs softly as Frankie urges her toward the bed.

They fall onto the bed together, arms and legs wrapped around each other, one body pressed against the other in a hot kiss. Frankie clamps her mouth against Alison's as she pushes her tongue between Alison's lips. Her hand finds one of Alison's breasts and she squeezes it, palpating the flesh, her mouth working against Alison's. The blonde croons with pleasure as Frankie pinches her nipple. Frankie moves her head down, moves her mouth to Alison's breasts. She takes the nipple she has just pinched, takes it between her lips and slowly drips her saliva over it. Does Alison understand how much she adores her?

Alison moans. "Kiss me everywhere."

Frankie's head is reeling with excitement as she wonders exactly what Alison means. Kiss me everywhere. The blonde's beauty intoxicates Frankie. Alison rolls from side to side on her back. So desirable. Frankie runs her hands over Alison's full breasts, over the nipples sticking up like darts. Alison's pink nipples are a provocation. Frankie bends to the feast, licking Alison's breasts, sucking each nipple in turn. Alison bends her head to watch Frankie's mouth. Frankie uses her hands to wiggle a breast against her lips. She's hungry for both nipples, annoyed she can't take them at the same time, two hard raisins so delicious that it makes her tremble. She gives them the full treatment, rubbing her face in the cleft between the two full breasts, rubbing her wet mouth over the nipples until they seem to swell into enormous berries. She inhales the scent of Alison's blonde skin.

Then Alison presses the top of Frankie's head. Frankie knows. She puts up no resistance to it. She rolls her face over Alison's diaphragm as she drags her mouth downward. There is no need for Alison to tell her what she wants. Frankie knows. She tugs at the waistband of Alison's panties.

"Pretty panties," Frankie says.

"Do you really like them?" The meaningless chatter of two lovers. Frankie presses her cheek against the nylon.

Alison wants to be sucked, and Alison, as usual, is tenacious. She pushes at Frankie's head again. Frankie pulls the panties down, tantalizing herself as she slowly uncovers more skin, the blonde bush, a thrill as she sees all of the triangle. What a lovely thick tuft she has! Alison lifts her ass to make the removal of the panties easier. Frankie pulls them off, sliding the wisp of nylon over Alison's nylon-clad legs, excited by the stockings that make Alison look so decadent. Alison lifts her knees, opening her thighs wide, then hooking one leg around Frankie to draw her in.

The blonde's meaty cunt is waiting like a pink clam. Frankie bends to it, bends to the eating of the clam as Alison moans with pleasure.

Before long Alison has both legs hooked around Frankie's back, her thighs wide apart, her cunt completely available to Frankie's mouth. Frankie uses her fingers to caress the outer lips. She wiggles the cunt with her fingertips, making the inner lips swell and open like petals. Alison's inner thighs are perfumed, and mixed with the perfume is the heady scent of her cunt. Frankie spreads the cunt wider, sniffing at it, wetting her nose with the blonde's syrup, nuzzling at the mouth of her vagina. Then she mashes her mouth against the cunt and she slurps in the velvet. Alison moans more loudly. Frankie strokes her tongue up and down, around in the hole and then licking upward to Alison's clitoris. The blonde's juices are flowing. Frankie nibbles at the lips, whips the clit with her tongue, and then sucks it between her lips as she twists her face in the wet swamp. Finally, she moves down to plunge her tongue inside the gaping vagina, her hands holding the larger lips apart, her tongue thrusting in and out rapidly, then stopping as she sucks the juices, then thrusting her tongue again. She knows how much Alison likes this. Alison has told her so. Frankie sucks up the juices, and then she bites one of the lips before burying her face in the clam again. Her desire is intense, suffocating, relentless. She feels Alison pulling at her hair, and she finally raises her head. The cunt, the haven, is now abandoned as Alison gazes at her with hot eyes.

Frankie's heart beats wildly as she watches Alison take hold of her breasts with her hands and give her a coy look. Frankie adores her. She has her now, but she wants even more of her.

Alison smiles and says, "Let me roll over." Ah, yes. Frankie backs away, and Alison rolls over onto her belly. Now Alison's lovely round ass is visible. She settles herself on the mattress with her thighs together, her buttocks tightly closed. Frankie's pulse races as she takes in the ass and the stockings, the firm full thighs tapering to the fine calves, then the beauty of Alison's ass again.

With a groan of desperate excitement, Frankie lowers her face to run her mouth over the curve of a springy buttock.

Alison whimpers, responding with a gentle wiggle of her hips.

Frankie treats the blonde's ass with reverence. She finds her own clitoris with her fingers and, as she slides her parted lips over Alison's buttock, she rubs the shaft of her clitoris with her fingertips.

She cherishes Alison's ass. She licks it with her wet tongue. The skin is like ivory, the flesh beneath it both firm and resilient, smooth and soft and warm. Frankie feels her own juices drizzling on her fingers as she moves to the other buttock.

Alison appears fascinated by Frankie's attentions. She whimpers, she bleats, she wriggles her ass under Frankie's face. They have done this before, and Frankie knows that Alison is fully aware how far it will go, how devoted Frankie can be, how loving to this part of her anatomy. "I like the way you do my ass," Alison once said. This made Frankie tremble with embarrassment, and she turned away hurriedly in order to hide her face.

Now Frankie manipulates both buttocks with her

hands. Alison responds to everything she does. The blonde moves her thighs apart, her skin catching the afternoon sunlight as she draws her knees forward a bit. This raises her ass, and as Frankie nuzzles in the crack, Alison moves her knees again and her ass lifts even farther.

Frankie is lost. Using both hands, she opens Alison's ass, pulls at the two loaves, pulls them apart even as she blushes at her own lust. But no one can see the blush. She buries her face between Alison's buttocks and moves her lips around as she kisses everywhere except the rosebud. The skin in the groove is soft and luscious and scented with Alison's perfume. Frankie cups Alison's cunt in her palm to feel the wetness, the wet heat of it. She slides her mouth down to the vaginal entrance now so blatantly exposed the opening gapes as a dark red hole.

With a groan, Alison arches her ass upward another few inches. Her knees slide farther apart, her thighs widening, her ass gently rolling.

Frankie's mind is in a whirl. It occurs to her that she'd rather have Alison in a garter belt. These stockings with elastic tops are sexy, but a garter belt would be more interesting. She wants the feel of garters under her fingertips as she presses her face into Alison's full ass. She tells herself that she needs to find a way to let Alison know, to whisper it sometime when Alison isn't expecting it. She imagines that Alison will be amused and say yes, she'll wear a garter belt if Frankie wants it.

Now Frankie gazes at the tendrils of hair in the crack. She holds Alison's hips as Alison writhes. She runs her thumbs along the inner slopes of Alison's buttocks, her fingers splayed to their full extent as she takes possession of Alison's ass. Below the split between the two buttocks, the pouch of Alison's cunt is a like a hairy mouth begging for attention.

Maybe sometime she'll have her on a boat, take her this way with the wind in the sails.

The counterpane on the bed is made of pink satin, now spotted in places with sweat and cunt syrup.

Both hands on Alison's ass, Frankie wiggles the cheeks, pulls the buttocks apart as she gazes at Alison's anus.

Frankie's clitoris feels swollen, enormous. She looks down at her belly and she wonders whether later on she'll have a chance to rub herself on Alison's ass and thighs. Alison is never predictable. The affair has its peaks and valleys. Frankie's head is now pounding with lust, her cunt oozing.

Alison elevates her ass even farther, offering it to Frankie, and now looking at Frankie over her shoulder. "Kiss me some more," Alison says.

Frankie becomes the lover commanded. She lowers her face again, nuzzling between Alison's buttocks. A great heat seems to radiate from the two globes. Frankie rubs her nipples against Alison's thighs, catching one nipple at the top of a stocking. She tries to remember what they did the last time. She wants their lovemaking to have enough variety to prevent Alison from getting bored. Now she slides her mouth over Alison's anus, wetting it, tickling it with her tongue, then placing her tongue directly on the ring and pushing just hard enough to make Alison feel it.

Alison moans. Frankie has a hand on her own cunt, her palm slowly rubbing her wet flesh, the wet mat of pubic hair. Does Alison realize how hot this makes her? For a brief moment, Frankie feels an urge to rebel against Alison's need to be serviced. This body worship. Frankie's cunt gushes in her hand,the syrup flowing over her fingers. Dear God, she's dripping. Alison bumps her ass upward. Frankie feels a tingling in her clitoris as she grips Alison's buttocks with her hands. Her tongue has now penetrated the tight ring, Alison groaning as she presses her ass back against Frankie's face. The blonde's thighs are wide apart, her back bent, her face turned to the side and pressed into the pillow, her eyes closed as she focuses all her attention on what Frankie is doing to her ass. For Frankie the caress is a violation, a possession, the heat in her chest rising as she plasters her lips against Alison's anus to suck it into a yielding softness.

Is the room too warm? The sweat seems to roll off Frankie's breasts in a torrent. She keeps her tongue active, sensitive to each cry of pleasure from Alison, probing vigorously and then relaxing to a mere delicate fluttering at the entrance.

When Alison finally comes, it's like the eruption of a volcano, her body quaking as Frankie suddenly transfers her hand from her own cunt to Alison's cunt, her fingers taking Alison's vagina, two fingers penetrating, thrusting deep inside the tunnel, sliding in and out as her tongue continues to wriggle in the blonde's receptive anus.

Afterward, after they bathe together and spread lotion over their bodies, Frankie makes love to Alison's ass again. Alison giggles and tells Frankie she's insatiable.

# FOURTEEN

# **Valerie**

When Frankie's law firm sends her to Washington for a few days, Valerie agrees to go dancing with Cleo in the evening. They go to a lesbian bar on Halsted, Valerie tingling with excitement and apprehension because it's possible someone who knows Frankie will see her with Cleo.

Once inside the crowded bar, Valerie's head becomes filled with the music, the noise, the press of so many women surrounding her. She hasn't had an evening out like this one in such a long time. She stands beside Cleo as Cleo waves to her friends, talks to her friends, ignoring Valerie who doesn't mind it because she doesn't want to be conspicuous. She's hoping that after they leave the bar, Cleo will take her home and give her a workout. Thinking about that makes Valerie shiver with excitement, the familiar excitement that occurs whenever she thinks of the

way Cleo handles her like a rag doll. Her syrup is
flowing. She can feel it. The ambience in the bar, the
rush, the noise, the mix of perfume turns her on.

Before long, a mannish-looking dyke swaggers
over to say hello to Cleo, and Valerie gets to meet
Pauly. They chat awhile, and then Cleo slides an arm
around Pauly's shoulders and smiles at Valerie.
"Pauly's an old friend, Val. You be nice to her while I
go say hello to someone."

Valerie is peeved, but there isn't much she can do
about it as Cleo walks off into the crowd. Pauly
presses against Valerie, presses her against the bar,
and says, "What'll you have, honey? You want another daiquiri?"

The play is there, Pauly playing her, running a
hand over Valerie's back at the same time as her knee
comes up to push through Valerie's dress against her
crotch. For a moment, Valerie wants to rebel, but she
finds that impossible. She realizes now that Cleo may
want this. The booze and the loud music make everything seem so wild. She wonders whether she ought
to keep away from Pauly. But no, Pauly won't have
that. Pauly moves in, kisses the side of her neck,
whispers into Valerie's ear that Valerie's breasts look
delicious in the low-cut dress, a real handful. "I like
tits," Pauly says as she turns to take another swig of
beer out the glass.

Just at that moment, a girl Valerie knows passes
them; the girl's eyes turning to look at them, the girl
smiling as she recognizes Valerie, raising an eyebrow,
then passing on without saying anything. Valerie
wonders whether the girl thinks she's with Pauly. Oh,
hell, Valerie thinks.

Pauly takes Valerie onto the dance floor. Pauly has
a strong body, and when she starts dancing, she looks
more mannish than ever. Valerie glances around the

crowded dance floor and she suddenly sees Cleo with a girl, a pretty blonde in a slinky dress, the two of them dancing. Valerie trembles with jealousy. She damns Cleo and Cleo's habit of making her look small.

Cleo seems mesmerized by the pretty blonde. The room is filled with gorgeous femmes, and now Valerie wonders why she ever agreed to this date with Cleo. She's not with Cleo anyway, she's with Pauly now. And she can tell that Pauly has an itch for her. That look in Pauly's eyes means that Pauly wants her in bed. Valerie imagines Pauly's thick fingers inside her cunt. Oh, yes, Pauly is coming onto her. Cleo obviously doesn't care one way or the other. Valerie tells herself that she means nothing to Cleo. Maybe that's why Cleo treats her like garbage. She continues dancing with Pauly, and now, as they shake their bodies past a mirror, Valerie looks at herself dancing with this big woman who wants to get inside her pants. She imagines it, imagines herself unrestrained with Pauly. What a mannish body she has; the way she moves, the way she tosses those strong arms around. Valerie feels helpless. Frankie is in Washington and Cleo is with another girl. She feels so alone, like a nothing little shadow of other women. That's all she is, a little shadow of Frankie and Cleo.

Pauly moves in now. As they dance, she puts her hands on Valerie's hips, her eyes fixed on Valerie's breasts almost popping out of the low-cut dress. "Let's go downstairs," Pauly says.

"Downstairs?"

"To the restroom, honey. Let's take a break and go downstairs, okay?"

Pauly leads her away. Valerie is thankful because she's tired of dancing and she needs the john anyway.

Pauly holds her with a strong arm around her waist as they make their way off the dance floor and down the stairs to where a line of women waits for the restroom to become available. Valerie and Pauly move into the line, Pauly standing behind Valerie with her crotch pressed against Valerie's ass and her mouth whispering in Valerie's ear as she tells Valerie she's the prettiest flower in the place, much prettier than any of the other femmes. Pauly whispers that she'd like to put it to her, get her dress up right there in the line and give it to her from behind with her fingers. Valerie quivers, excited by Pauly now even though she didn't expect it. The image of Pauly fucking her from behind is exciting. Pauly is different than Cleo and Frankie, more determined, more confident. Valerie feels the big woman radiating sex behind her like a hot oven.

Finally Valerie and Pauly are up at the front of the line. Before long they get their turn, and they move into the restroom together. Valerie immediately moves to one of the empty stalls, but then she feels an immediate shock as Pauly pushes behind her into the stall, Pauly locking the door and then grabbing Valerie and kissing her mouth, Pauly's hand sliding under Valerie's dress to get at her cunt, the older woman's thick fingers taking possession of Valerie without any preliminaries.

Valerie gasps. "My God, stop it!"

But Pauly only chuckles. "Come on, baby, give it to mama."

She makes Valerie open her legs farther, and as soon as Valerie does this, Pauly's fingers are in there more insistent than ever, two fingers and then three fingers pushing inside Valerie's wet cunt, Valerie groaning and finally lifting one foot to the commode to make it easier for Pauly to get her off. It doesn't take long, not with a dyke as skillful as Pauly, and soon Valerie is shuddering as the hot pleasure rips through her body. After the first orgasm, Valerie begs Pauly to stop, but instead Pauly makes Valerie turn around and put her hands on the toilet tank. Pauly now raises Valerie's dress, strokes her ass, and then quickly gets her fingers inside Valerie's cunt again, this time from the rear.

Valerie is ravished. She can't stop it now because the pleasure is too sharp. The insides of her thighs are drenched all the way down to the tops of her stockings. She groans and gasps, praying that no one outside the stall will hear her. Pauly renews the attack, a fierce fucking in Valerie's cunt with her fingers, and then at last Pauly gets her thumb in Valerie's ass and Pauly says, "Cleo told me you're a hot ass. Yeah, she's right, isn't she?"

In the midst of the wild orgasm, Valerie understands what has happened; understands that Cleo has dumped her, thrown her away, given her to Pauly to be Pauly's dolly.

Valerie comes hard, crying at the same time, sobbing her desperation, and of course Pauly thinks that the sobbing means Valerie is in heaven.

Oh God, I don't want this, Valerie thinks. This is not what she wants. She hates Pauly, she hates Cleo, she hates everything that's happened to her. She wants Frankie back. Oh, yes, she wants Frankie.

# FIFTEEN

# **Frankie**

Frankie is sitting alone in a restaurant on Chestnut Street, waiting for Alison, fidgeting with her napkin. She has been back in Chicago three days, and all she cares about now is seeing Alison again. The trip to Washington was dull, or maybe her mind these days just isn't focused enough on her work. What she feels at the moment is anxiety. And sexual expectation. She hopes Alison will be free this afternoon. Frankie wriggles on the chair, wondering whether her skirt is wrinkled. Under the tailored jacket she wears a white shirt without a bra, and she can feel the texture of the cloth against her nipples. She looks around the room and feels her sexual hunger again. Will she ever be content? When she was a girl, she always thought a full moon so romantic, and what was more important in life than romance? Now she knows that it's not romance that's important, it's love. Intense absorbing love. She had that once with Valerie, but maybe it will never return. She had such a difficult time getting Alison to meet her today. For an instant Frankie wonders whether maybe Alison is too fickle. Maybe she doesn't care enough. What a pity to meet her in a restaurant and not be able to hug her when they see each other. Play tough, Frankie thinks, always play tough. Alison irritated her yesterday by her coyness about meeting today. She's too beautiful, Frankie thinks. She wants her fingers inside Alison. I'm living on hope, Frankie thinks. She lives on the hope that things will work out for her, that her life will get settled somehow. What does she want? Does she want Alison or Valerie? Is one woman enough? There are things about Valerie that still excite her immensely. Her legs, for instance. But Alison excites her, too. The way Alison purrs when Frankie gropes her. The way Alison likes to offer her ass. Maybe it's the subtlety. Alison is more subtle than Valerie. You don't understand anything, Frankie thinks. She understands torts and estates, but she has no understanding of what she wants from women. She's mystified.

Finally Alison arrives, a tall, graceful vision entering the room, looking around, spotting Frankie, walking toward her. Frankie feels the hunger again, an intense desire to taste Alison's beauty.

"Hi," Alison says, a soft smile as she sits down opposite Frankie.

"You look wonderful," Frankie says. And then she adds, "I missed you terribly."

Alison accepts the token of affection with a demure glance. She picks up the menu and begins discussing it, what she likes, what she doesn't like. She says she hasn't been in this restaurant in some time and she isn't that certain about the food. Frankie has no interest in the food; all she cares about is Alison, the memories of them together, the sequence of erotic images now passing through her mind one after the other, each image singeing her brain before it vanishes only to be replaced by another image. What do I want? Frankie thinks. At the moment, what she wants is the feel of her chin pushing at Alison's cunt, Alison's juices dribbling on her chin. The memory makes Frankie tremble. She tells herself that she must stop it before she destroys herself.

Alison is different. Frankie senses a change in Alison. They talk about Frankie's trip to Washington, but Alison seems uninterested. She looks at her hands, at her long fingers. Frankie talks, but as she talks, she schemes about how to get Alison into bed this afternoon. She wants Alison in her arms. She imagines herself kissing Alison, petting her, yielding to the desire Alison has to have Frankie's tongue everywhere. Frankie's tongue and nose. A memory of Alison's scent is suddenly so vivid that Frankie shudders with delight. Scintillating.

Then Alison says, "We need to talk about something."

"What?"

"Something important."

"I'm listening." Frankie tells herself that Alison's ass is so perfect, so breathtaking. And her belly. And the way she comes.

Alison says, "I've decided I can't go on with this. I really can't."

"What do you mean?"

"I'm talking about us. I'm sorry."

Frankie remembers Alison moaning as she hunches up to get more of Frankie's fingers.

"Just like that?"

Alison looks away. "Don't you think it's better to be more direct? I think it's much better."

For a moment Frankie thinks there might be some way to pacify Alison, something Alison wants, anything. But of course it's a mirage.

Frankie says, "Why?"

Alison shrugs. "I've decided I don't want the circumstances."

"You don't want a gay life?"

Nervous, Alison looks around to see whether anyone has heard. "Yes, that's it."

"Oh, shit!" Frankie says.

Alison blushes. "I was hoping we'd stay friends."

Frankie looks at her. She says nothing. And then she puts her napkin on the table and rises. "I'll take care of the check on the way out. Good-bye, Alison."

In her office in the afternoon, Frankie's mood alternates between rage and sadness and frustration. Sexual frustration. She understands that with Alison it was more sex than anything else. Even thinking about Alison now causes her juices to flow. She wanted to be with Alison this afternoon, and now instead it's over, Alison gone from her life, the affair ended. How can I be so stupid? Frankie thinks. The only bedrock in her life is Valerie. Loyal Valerie. Oh, yes.

Frankie leaves the office early and goes to Bloomingdale's. Inside the store, she passes a mirror and stops to stare at herself. Well-groomed young female attorney who might be a dyke but who might not. What's her niche? She brushes a fleck of lint off her thigh. Then she finds the lingerie department, and she buys a black negligée and she has it gift-wrapped. Is the salesgirl wondering who the gift is for?

"Would you like a card?"

"No, that's not necessary."

The girl gives Frankie a smug smile. Frankie thinks

of something to say, but rather than prolong the farce, she takes her package and leaves. Some women are such rotten bitches, so bitchy they can't be answered.

In the evening, Frankie kisses Valerie. "Have a nice day?"

Valerie shrugs. "Not much of anything."

"I missed you."

Valerie whimpers. "You did?"

Frankie kisses her again, her tongue sliding over Valerie's mouth. "I bought you a present."

"You did?"

Frankie brings her the Bloomingdale's box, and she sits and watches Valerie as Valerie giggles and hurries to open the box.

She's beautiful, Frankie thinks. She's more beautiful than Alison.

Valerie moans with joy as she pulls out the black negligée. "Oh Frankie!"

"Do you like it?"

"I love it! I'll try it on, okay?"

"Sure." While Valerie is gone, Frankie turns on some music and pours out two glasses of white wine. Pity she hadn't thought of champagne. She closes the blinds and turns down some of the lights in the living room. She's eager now, all the anger and pain of the afternoon washed away, the only thought in her mind the next few hours with Valerie.

My only love, Frankie thinks. Valerie comes into the room wearing the black negligée and high heels, blushing, her dark triangle visible through the sheer folds.

"I love you," Valerie says.

And Frankie says, "Come over here and kiss me."

People are talking about:

# The Masquerade
# Erotic Newsletter

◆ ◆ ◆ ◆ ◆ ◆ ◆ ◆ ◆ ◆ ◆ ◆ ◆ ◆ ◆ ◆ ◆ ◆ ◆

FICTION, ESSAYS, REVIEWS, PHOTOGRAPHY,
INTERVIEWS, EXPOSÉS, AND MUCH MORE!

◆ ◆ ◆ ◆ ◆ ◆ ◆ ◆ ◆ ◆ ◆ ◆ ◆ ◆ ◆ ◆ ◆ ◆ ◆

"I received the new issue of the newsletter; it looks better and better."
—*Michael Perkins*

"I must say that yours is a nice little magazine, literate and intelligent."
—*HH, Great Britain*

"Fun articles on writing porn and about the peep shows, great for those of us who will probably never step onto a strip stage or behind the glass of a booth, but love to hear about it, wicked little voyeurs that we all are, hm? Yes indeed...."
—*MT, California*

"Many thanks for your newsletter with essays on various forms of eroticism. Especially enjoyed your new Masquerade collections of books dealing with gay sex."
—*GF, Maine*

"... a professional, insider's look at the world of erotica ..."
—*SCREW*

"I recently received a copy of **The Masquerade Erotic Newsletter**. I found it to be quite informative and interesting. The intelligent writing and choice of subject matter are refreshing and stimulating. You are to be congratulated for a publication that looks at different forms of eroticism without leering or smirking."
—*DP, Connecticut*

"Thanks for sending the books and the two latest issues of **The Masquerade Erotic Newsletter**. Provocative reading, I must say."
—*RH, Washington*

"Thanks for the latest copy of **The Masquerade Erotic Newsletter**. It is a real stunner."
—*CJS, New York*

## *Free* GIFT

### WHEN YOU SUBSCRIBE TO:
# The Masquerade Erotic Newsletter

Receive two **MASQUERADE** books of your choice

# THE MASQUERADE EROTIC LIBRARY

## ROSEBUD BOOKS
### $4.95 each

**PRIVATE LESSONS**                      *Lindsay Welsh*

A high voltage tale of life at The Whitfield Academy for Young Women—where cruel headmistress Devon Whitfield presides over the in-depth education of only the most talented and delicious of maidens. Elizabeth Dunn arrives at the Academy, where it becomes clear that she has much to learn—to the delight of Devon Whitfield and her randy staff of Mistresses in Residence!         **3116-0**

**BAD HABITS**                            *Lindsay Welsh*

What does one do with a poorly trained slave? Break her of her bad habits, of course! When a respected dominatrix notices the poor behavior displayed by her slave, she decides to open a school: one where submissives will learn the finer points of servitude—and learn them properly. "If you like hot, lesbian erotica, run—don't walk ... and pick up a copy of *Bad Habits* ..."     —Karen Bullock-Jordan, *Lambda Book Report*. **3068-7**

**PROVINCETOWN SUMMER**              *Lindsay Welsh*

This completely original collection is devoted exclusively to white-hot desire between women.From the casual encounters of women on the prowl to the enduring erotic bond between old lovers, the women of *Provincetown Summer* will set your senses on fire! A nationally bestselling title.         **3040-7**

**MISTRESS MINE**                     *Valentina Cilescu*

Sophia Cranleigh sits in prison, accused of authoring the "obscene" *Mistress Mine*. She is offered salvation—with the condition that she first relate her lurid life story. For Sophia has led no ordinary life, but has slaved and suffered—deliciously—under the hand of the notorious Mistress Malin. Sophia tells her story, never imagining the way in which she'd be repaid for her honesty....         **109-8**

**LEATHERWOMEN**                *edited by Laura Antoniou*

A groundbreaking anthology. These fantasies, from the pens of new or emerging authors, break every rule imposed on women's fantasies, telling stories of the secret extremes so many dream of. The hottest stories from some of today's newest and most outrageous writers make this an unforgettable exploration of the female libido.         **3095-4**

**PASSAGE AND OTHER STORIES**            *Aarona Griffin*

An S/M romance. Lovely Nina is frightened by her lesbian passions until she finds herself infatuated with a woman she spots at a local café. One night Nina follows her and finds herself enmeshed in an endless maze leading to a mysterious world where women test the edges of sexuality and power.   **3057-1**

**DISTANT LOVE & OTHER STORIES**             *A.L. Reine*

In the title story, Leah Michaels and her lover Ranelle have had four years of blissful, smoldering passion together. One night, when Ranelle is out of town, Leah records an audio "Valentine," a cassette filled with erotic reminiscences of their life together in vivid, pulsating detail.         **3056-3**

# EROTIC PLAYGIRL ROMANCES
## $4.95 each

**WOMEN AT WORK**                                          *Charlotte Rose*

Hot, uninhibited stories devoted to the working woman! From a lonesome cowgirl to a supercharged public relations exec, these uncontrollable women know how to let off steam after a tough day on the job. Career pursuits pale beside their devotion to less professional pleasures, as each proves that "moonlighting" is often the best job of all!          **3088-1**

**LOVE & SURRENDER**                                        *Marlene Darcy*

"Madeline saw Harry looking at her legs and she blushed as she remembered what he wanted to do.... She casually pulled the skirt of her dress back to uncover her knees and the lower part of her thighs. What did he want now? Did he want more? She tugged at her skirt again, pulled it back far enough so almost all of her thighs were exposed...."          **3082-2**

**THE COMPLETE *PLAYGIRL* FANTASIES**

The very best—and very hottest—women's fantasies are collected here, fresh from the pages of Playgirl. These knockouts from the infamous "Reader's Fantasy Forum" prove, once again, that truth can indeed be hotter, wilder, and better than fiction.          **3075-X**

**DREAM CRUISE**                                          *Gwenyth James*

Angelia has it all—a brilliant career and a beautiful face to match. But she longs to kick up her high heels and have some fun, so she takes an island vacation and vows to leave her sexual inhibitions behind. From the moment her plane takes off, she finds herself in one hot and steamy encounter after another, and her horny holiday doesn't end on Monday morning! Rest and relaxation were never so rewarding.          **3045-0**

# RHINOCEROS BOOKS
## $6.95 each

**RHINOCEROS ANTHOLOGY OF CLASSIC ANONYMOUS EROTIC WRITING**          Edited by Michael Perkins

Michael Perkins, acclaimed authority on erotic literature, has collected the very best passages from the world's erotic writing—especially for Rhinoceros readers. "Anonymous" is one of the most infamous bylines in publishing history—and these steamy excerpts show why! Well-crafted and arousing reading for porn connoisseurs. Available only from Rhinoceros Books.          **140-3**

**THE REPENTENCE OF LORRAINE**                            *Andrei Codrescu*

An aspiring writer, a professor's wife, a secretary, gold anklets, Maoists, Roman harlots—and more—swirl through this spicy tale of a harried quest for a mythic artifact. Written when the author was a young man, this lusty yarn was inspired by the heady—and hot—days and nights of the Sixties. A rare title from this perenially popular and acclaimed author, finally back in print.          **124-1**

**THE WET FOREVER**                                      *David Aaron Clark*

The story of Janus and Madchen—a small-time hood and a beautiful sex worker—The Wet Forever examines themes of loyalty, sacrifice, redemption and obsession amidst Manhattan's sex parlors and underground S/M clubs.. Its combination of sex and suspense makes The Wet Forever singular, uncompromising, and strangely arousing.          **117-9**

**ORF** *David Meltzer*

He is the ultimate musician-hero—the idol of thousands, the fevered dream of many more. And like many musicians before him, he is misunderstood, misused—and totally out of control. From agony to lust, every last drop of feeling is squeezed from a modern-day troubadour and his lady love on their relentless descent into hell. Long out of print, Meltzer's frank, poetic look at the dark side of the Sixties returns. A masterpiece—and a must for every serious erotic library. **110-1**

**MANEATER** *Sophie Galleymore Bird*

Through a bizarre act of creation, a man attains the "perfect" lover—by all appearances a beautiful, sensuous woman but in reality something far darker. Once brought to life she will accept no mate, seeking instead the prey that will sate her supernatural hunger for vengeance. A biting take on the war of the sexes, this stunning debut novel goes for the jugular of the "perfect woman" myth. **103-9**

**VENUS IN FURS** *Leopold von Sacher-Masoch*

This classic 19th century novel is the first uncompromising exploration of the dominant/submissive relationship in literature. The alliance of Severin and Wanda epitomizes Sacher-Masoch's dark obsession with a cruel, controlling goddess and the urges that drive the man held in her thrall. Also included in this volume are the letters exchanged between Sacher-Masoch and Emilie Mataja—an aspiring writer he sought as the avatar of his forbidden desires. **3089-X**

## ALICE JOANOU

**TOURNIQUET** **3067-9**

A brand new collection of stories and effusions from the pen of one our most dazzling young writers. By turns lush and austere, Joanou's intoxicating command of language and image makes *Tourniquet* a sumptuous feast for all the senses. From the writer *Screw* credited with making "the most impressive erotic debut in many a moon."

**CANNIBAL FLOWER** **72-6**

"She is waiting in her darkened bedroom, as she has waited throughout history, to seduce and ultimately destroy the men who are foolish enough to be blinded by her irresistible charms. She is Salome, Lucrezia Borgia, Delilah—endlessly alluring, the fulfillment of your every desire.... She is the goddess of sexuality, and *Cannibal Flower* is her haunting siren song." —Michael Perkins

## MICHAEL PERKINS

**EVIL COMPANIONS** **3067-9**

A handsome edition of this cult classic that includes a new preface by Samuel R. Delany. Set in New York City during the tumultuous waning years of the 60s, *Evil Companions* has been hailed as "a frightening classic." A young couple explore the nether reaches of the erotic unconscious in a shocking confrontation with the extremes of passion. About *Evil Companions*, Thomas M. Disch said "Michael Perkins is America's answer to de Sade ... by comparison to this book, Bret Easton Ellis' *American Psycho* is only a lesson in good grooming...."

**THE SECRET RECORD: Modern Erotic Literature** **3039-3**

Michael Perkins, a renowned author and critic of sexually explicit fiction, surveys the field with authority and unique insight. Updated and revised to include the latest trends, tastes, and developments in this much-misunderstood and maligned genre. An important nonfiction volume for every erotic reader aand fan of high quality adult fiction, *The Secret Record* is finally back in print.

**SENSATIONS** *Tuppy Owens*

A piece of porn history. Tuppy Owens tells the unexpurgated story of the making of *Sensations*—the first big-budget sex flick. Originally commissioned to appear in book form after the release of the film in 1975, *Sensations* is finally released under Masquerade's stylish Rhino*ceros* imprint. A document from a more reckless, bygone time! **3081-4**

**THE MARKETPLACE** *Sara Adamson*

"Merchandise does not come easily to the Marketplace.... They haunt the clubs and the organizations, their need so real and desperate that they exude sensual tension when they glide through the crowds. Some of them are so ripe that they intimidate the poseurs, the weekend sadists and the furtive dilettantes who are so endemic to that world. And they never stop asking where we may be found...." A compelling tale of the ultimate training academy, where only the finest are accepted—and trained for service beyond their wildest dreams. **3096-2**

**MY DARLING DOMINATRIX** *Grant Antrews*

When a man and a woman fall in love it's supposed to be simple, uncomplicated, easy—unless that woman happens to be a dominatrix. Devoid of sleaze and shame, this honest and unpretentious love story captures the richness and depth of this very special kind of love. Rare and undeniably unique. **3055-5**

**ILLUSIONS** *Daniel Vian*

Two disturbing tales of danger and desire on the eve of WWII. From private homes to lurid cafés to decaying streets, passion is explored, exposed, and placed in stark contrast to the brutal violence of the time. *Illusions* peels the frightened mask from the face of desire, and studies its changing features under the dim lights of a lonely Berlin evening. Two unforgettable and evocative stories. **3074-1**

**LOVE IN WARTIME** *Liesel Kulig*

Madeleine knew that the handsome SS officer was a dangerous man. But she was just a cabaret singer in Nazi-occupied Paris, trying to survive in a perilous time. When Josef fell in love with her, he discovered that a beautiful and amoral woman can sometimes be wildly dangerous. **3044-X**

## MASQUERADE BOOKS
### $4.95 each

**THE EROTIC ADVENTURES OF HARRY TEMPLE** *Anonymous*

The first book of libertine Harry Temple's memoirs chronicles his amorous adventures from his initiation at the hands of two insatiable sirens, through his apprenticeship at a house of hot repute, to his encounters with a nymphomaniac in a chastity belt and other twisted partners. **127-6**

**PAULINE** *Anonymous*

From rural America to the Franfurt Opera House to the royal court of Austria, Pauline follows her ever growing sexual desires. "They knew not that I was a prima donna, sought after by royalty, indulged and petted by the elite of all Europe. I would never see them again. Why shouldn't I give myself to them that they might become more and more inspired to deeds of greater lust!" A sexy diva takes on all comers. **129-2**

**ODD WOMEN** *Rachel Perez*

These women are lots of things: sexy, smart, innocent, tough—some even say odd. But who cares, when their combined ass-ettes are so sweet! There's not a moral in sight as an assortment of Sapphic sirens proves once and for all that comely ladies come best in pairs. **123-3**

## AFFINITIES *Rachel Perez*

"Kelsy had a liking for cool upper-class blondes, the long- legged girls from Lake Forest and Winnetka who came into the city to cruise the lesbian bars on Halsted, looking for breathless ecstasies. Kelsy thought of them as icebergs that needed melting, these girls with a quiet demeanor and so much under the surface...." **3113-6**

## JENNIFER *Anonymous*

From the bedroom of an internationally famous—and notoriously insatiable—dancer to an uninhibited ashram, Jennifer traces the exploits of one thoroughly modern woman. Moving beyond mere sexual experimentation, Jennifer slowly comes to a new realization of herself—as a passionate woman whose hungers are as boundless as they are diverse. Nothing stops the insatiable Jennifer! **107-1**

## HELLFIRE *Charles G. Wood*

A vicious murderer is running amok in New York's sexual underground—and Nick O'Shay, a virile detective with the NYPD, plunges deep into the case. He soon becomes embroiled in an elusive world of fleshly extremes, hunting a madman seeking to purge America with fire and blood sacrifices. But the rules are different here, as O'Shay soon discovers on his journey through every sexual extreme—and his ultimate encounter with the ugly face of repression. **3085-7**

## ROSEMARY LANE *J.D. Hall*

The ups, downs, ins and outs of Rosemary Lane, an 18th century maiden named after the street in which she was abandoned as a child. Raised as the ward of Lord and Lady D'Arcy, after coming of age she discovers that her guardians' generosity is truly boundless—as they contribute heartily to her carnal education. **3078-4**

## HELOISE *Sarah Jackson*

A panoply of sensual tales harkening back to the golden age of Victorian erotica. Desire is examined in all its intricacy, as fantasies are explored and urges explode. Innocence meets experience time and again in these passionate stories dedicated to the pleasures of the body. Sweetly torrid tales of erotic awakening abound in this volume devoted to the deepest sexual explorations. **3073-3**

## MASTER OF TIMBERLAND *Sara H. French*

"Welcome to Timberland Resort," he began. "We are delighted that you have come to serve us. And you may all be assured that we will require service of you in the strictest sense. Our discipline is the most demanding in the world. You will be trained here by the best. And now your new Masters will make their choices." Luscious slaves serve in the ultimate vacation paradise. **3059-8**

## GARDEN OF DELIGHT *Sydney St. James*

A vivid account of sexual awakening that follows an innocent but insatiably curious young woman's journey from the furtive, forbidden joys of dormitory life to the unabashed carnality of the wild world. Pretty Pauline blossoms with each new experiment in the sensual arts—until finally nothing can contain her extravagant desires. **3058-X**

## STASI SLUT *Anthony Bobarzynski*

Adina lives in East Germany, far from the sexually liberated, uninhibited debauchery of the West. She meets a group of ruthless and corrupt STASI agents who use her as a pawn in their political chess game as well as for their own gratification—until she uses her undeniable talents and attractions in a final bid for total freedom in the revolutionary climax of this Red-hot thriller! **3052-0**

**BLUE TANGO**  *Hilary Manning*

Ripe and tempting Julie is haunted by the sounds of extraordinary passion beyond her bedroom wall. Alone, she fantasizes about taking part in the amorous dramas of her hosts, Claire and Edward. When she finds a way to watch the nightly debauch, her curiosity turns to full-blown lust and the uncontrollable Julie goes wild with desire!  **3037-7**

**THE CATALYST**  *Sara Adamson*

After viewing a controversial, explicitly kinky film full of images of bondage and submission, several audience members find themselves deeply moved by the erotic suggestions they've seen on the screen. Each inspired coupling explores their every imagined extreme, as long-denied urges explode with new intensity.  **3015-6**

**LUST**  *Palmiro Vicarion*

A wealthy and powerful man of leisure recounts his rise up the corporate ladder and his corresponding descent into debauchery. Adventure and political intrigue provide a stimulating backdrop for this tale of a classic scoundrel with an uncurbed appetite for sexual power!  **82-3**

**WAYWARD**  *Peter Jason*

A mysterious countess hires a tour bus for an unusual vacation. Traveling through Europe's most notorious cities, she picks up friends, lovers, and acquaintances from every walk of life in pursuit of unbridled sensual pleasure. Each guest brings unique sexual tastes and talents to the group, climaxing in countless orgies, outrageous acts, endless deviation—and a trip none would forget!  **3004-0**

**ASK ISADORA**  *Isadora Alman*

Six years of collected columns on sex and relationships. Syndicated columnist Alman has been called a hip Dr. Ruth and a sexy Dear Abby. Her advice is sharp, funny, and pertinent to anyone experiencing the delights and dilemmas of being a sexual creature in today's perplexing world.  **61-0**

## LOUISE BELHAVEL

### FORBIDDEN DELIGHTS

Clara and Iris make their sexual debut in this chronicle of the forbidden. Sexual taboos are what turn this pair on, as they travel the globe in search of the next erotic threshold. The effect they have on their fellow world travelers is definitely contagious!  **81-5**

### FRAGRANT ABUSES

The saga of Clara and Iris continues as the now-experienced girls enjoy themselves with a new circle of worldly friends whose imaginations definitely match their own. Polymorphous perversity follows the lusty ladies around the globe!  **88-2**

### DEPRAVED ANGELS

The final installment in the incredible adventures of Clara and Iris. Together with their friends, lovers, and worldly acquaintances, Clara and Iris explore the frontiers of depravity at home and abroad.  **92-0**

## TITIAN BERESFORD

### A TITIAN BERESFORD READER

A captivating collection! Beresford's fanciful settings and outrageous fetishism have established his reputation as one of modern erotica's most imaginative and spirited writers. Wildly cruel dominatrixes, deliciously perverse masochists, and mesmerizing detail are the hallmarks of the Beresford tale—the best of which are collected here for the first time.  **3114-4**

## CINDERELLA

Titian Beresford triumphs again with castle dungeons and tightly corseted ladies-in-waiting, naughty viscounts and impossibly cruel masturbatrixes—nearly every conceivable method of erotic torture is explored and described in lush, vivid detail.                                    3024-5

## JUDITH BOSTON

Young Edward would have been lucky to get the stodgy old companion he thought his parents had hired for him. Instead, an exqusite woman arrives at his door, and Edward finds his compulsively lewd behavior never goes unpunished by the unflinchingly severe Judith Boston!                       87-4

## CHINA BLUE

### KUNG FU NUNS

"When I could stand the pleasure no longer, she lifted me out of the chair and sat me down on top of the table. She then lifted her skirt. The sight of her perfect legs clad in white stockings and a petite garter belt further mesmerized me. I lean particularly towards white garter belts."          3031-8

### SECRETS OF THE CITY

China Blue, the infamous Madame of Saigon, a black belt enchantress in the martial arts of love, is out for revenge. Her search brings her to Manhattan, where she intends to call upon her secret sexual arts to kill her enemies at the height of ecstasy.                                            03-3

## HARRIET DAIMLER

### DARLING • INNOCENCE

In Darling, a virgin is raped by a mugger. Driven by her urge for revenge, she searches New York for him in a furious sexual hunt that leads to rape and murder. In Innocence, a young invalid determines to experience sex through her voluptuous nurse. Two critically acclaimed novels in one extraordinary volume.                                                   3047-4

### THE PLEASURE THIEVES

They are the Pleasure Thieves, whose sexually preoccupied targets are set up by luscious Carol Stoddard. She forms an ultra-hot sexual threesome with them, trying every combination from two-on-ones to daisy chains—but always on the sly, because pleasures are even sweeter when they're stolen!                                                           036-X

## AKBAR DEL PIOMBO

### SKIRTS

Randy Mr. Edward Champdick enters high society—and a whole lot more—in his quest for ultimate satisfaction. For it seems that once Mr. Champdick rises to the occasion, almost nothing can bring him down. Nothing, that is, except continual, indiscriminate sexual gratification under the nearest skirt.                                                      3115-2

### DUKE COSIMO

A kinky, lighthearted romp of non-stop action is played out against the boudoirs, bathrooms and ballrooms of the European nobility, who seem to do nothing all day except each other.                                     3052-0

### A CRUMBLING FAÇADE

The return of that incorrigible rogue, Henry Pike,who continues his pursuit of sex, fair or otherwise, in the most elegant homes of the most irreproachable and debauched aristocrats. No one can resist the irrespressible Pike—especially when he's on the prowl.                               3043-1

# ORDERING IS EASY!

MC/VISA orders can be placed by calling our toll-free number

**PHONE 800-458-9640 / FAX 212 986-7355**

or mail the coupon below to:

**Masquerade Books 801 Second Avenue New York, New York. 10017**

## BUY ANY FOUR BOOKS AND CHOOSE ONE ADDITIONAL BOOK AS YOUR FREE GIFT.

| QTY. | TITLE | L 124-1 | NO. | PRICE |
|------|-------|---------|-----|-------|
|      |       |         |     |       |
|      |       |         |     |       |
|      |       |         |     |       |
|      |       |         |     |       |
|      |       |         |     |       |
|      |       |         |     |       |
|      |       |         |     |       |
|      |       |         |     |       |
|      |       |         |     |       |
|      |       |         |     |       |
|      |       | SUBTOTAL |    |       |
|      |       | POSTAGE & HANDLING | |    |
|      |       | **TOTAL** |   |       |

Add $1.00 Postage and Handling for tthe first book and 50¢ for each additional book. Outside the U.S. add $2.00 for the first book, $1.00 for each additional book. New York state residents add 8-1/4% sales tax.

**NAME** _____

**ADDRESS** _____ **APT. #** _____

**CITY** _____ **STATE** _____ **ZIP** _____

**TEL. (      )** _____

**PAYMENT:** ☐ CHECK ☐ MONEY ORDER ☐ VISA ☐ MC

**CARD NO.** _____ **EXP. DATE** _____

PLEASE ALLOW 4–6 WEEKS DELIVERY. NO C.O.D. ORDERS. PLEASE MAKE ALL CHECKS PAYABLE TO MASQUERADE BOOKS. PAYABLE IN U.S. CURRENCY ONLY